HURRICANES
&
HANGOVERS

And Other Tall Tales & Loose Lies
From the Coconut Telegraph

By Dear Miss Mermaid

Dedication

"Hurricanes & Hangovers"
is dedicated in loving memory of:

Marian Fairchild Gill, who taught me to read.

Bill Janis, who taught me to laugh.

Lil Steve Bunner, who taught me to heal.

And Sharon Ward, who taught me to live.

May you all, Rest in Peace.

Your profound influence and love,
forever changed my life.

Dear Miss Mermaid

Cover Design by BookSurge Design Consultants
(BookSurge.Com)

Visit DearMissMermaid.Com or BookSurge.Com To Order
Additional Copies

Published by This Old Pirate Po Box 1533 St John VI 00831

ISBN: 1-4196-5532-9
ISBN-13: 9781419655326

Table of Contents

Preface

Ahoy pirates, mermaids, sailors and landlubbers! This little book you hold in your hand is just what the captain ordered! Let this highly entertaining collection of humorous tales carry you away to a wacky world where life is a bubble or two off center and all boats list lightly to portside. Each one of these wild and bawdy Caribbean tales will keep you smiling all day long. Loosely based on fact, many of the names of places and people have been changed (to protect the guilty, of course). But the flavor is definitely Caribbean and the laughs are universal.

You won't regret plunging into the cool pages of this red-hot book. Unforgettable, original characters serve up a fine feast of island life, replete with laid-back sea-to-shore attitudes and spicy inimitable Caribbean spirit. So put on your sunglasses, pick up a nice cold drink, and lay back in your deck chair. Let these tall tales and loose lies melt your troubles away in the uncharted waters of fun.

Editor
Linda K. Palmer

Traffic Lights

Downtown they installed a brand new traffic light! The first ever on Tortola. I observed with wonder the first time that they turned it on. The timing was a bit off. First, the light was red in all four directions. Then it turned green in all four directions! Finally, the road engineers reset the light to flashing yellow in all four directions and installed a policeman to direct the traffic.

The poor policeman was in death's pathway the entire day. We could hear screeching tires every few seconds, because folks here know nothing about traffic lights and rarely ever see a policeman directing traffic either. Tortola drivers go and stop as they please, as everyone knows. The poor man must have been low on the police totem pole to draw such an assignment, or else they did it as a joke because he was new on the beat. He was dodging cars left and right like a matador in a ring with a dozen wild bulls.

I recall another time when there was a big traffic snarl in town. I stopped in one of the bars to have a drink, figuring I would relax until the traffic cleared. A policeman came in to order a cold drink, and someone asked him why he wasn't directing traffic to ease the snarl.

He replied, "WHAT? The folks here drive real crazy, mon! I could get killed doing that!"

So, now that we have a new traffic light on our island, every day on the local radio station for an hour they give instructions on how to use the traffic light and what all those pretty colors mean. I am starting a betting pool on how many wrecks and mash-ups we have the first week it is in operation.

You see, it must have been someone from off-island who came up with this lamebrain idea for a traffic light. A Tortolian would know better than to introduce something so foolish! WHY? Because Tortolians like to do as they please. To do anything less is a serious loss of freedom. Drivers here stop in the middle of the road to talk with pedestrians, to pickup and discharge hitchhikers, to fix the carburetor, or to wash the car. Wash the car?? Yes! I had to drive up on the sidewalk one day to get around a car that was parked in the street blocking traffic while being washed. How does a traffic light help ease that problem?

Drivers here often stop in the middle of the road to run inside a store or business. They may stay gone for 20 minutes while the traffic just backs up behind them. Can a traffic light help out with that?

I've seen folks park their cars in the road, blocking the entrance to a parking lot!

One time I stopped at a store in West End that has a parking lot that accommodates about 20 cars. When I pulled in, there was not a car in sight. I parked neatly (unheard of around here!). When I came out, there were a total of three cars in the parking lot—mine and the two that were blocking me. The expansive parking lot spread out vacantly around us. Those two other cars must have been so lonely that they had to snuggle up to mine like three puppies sleeping on top of each other—a little jumbled pile of puppy/cars in the middle of a big, spread-out blanket/parking-lot.

Well, they tested the traffic light a second time. It caused major congestion. So they turned it back off. The congestion cleared up.

This week's newspaper has been running a quarter-page illustration explaining how to read the traffic lights. The only problem is that the article is being printed in black and white. The lack of color doesn't quite convey the essential elements in the traffic light situation. You know, those red, yellow, and green elements.

The article displays a photograph of a traffic signal with the top light blacked out. The caption says this means, "STOP." Underneath this, the ad shows a second photograph of a traffic light with the middle light in black. The caption explains you should stop if you have not crossed the line at the intersection. Then it shows a blacked-out bottom light and says this means, "GO."

Typical Tortolian style...

Although other remote locations may have similar difficulties when modern amenities arrive.

Vernon in Vieques wrote me: "What is a traffic light? Vieques [a tiny island off Puerto Rico] doesn't have traffic lights either."

Well, Vernon, you are not alone. Over half of Tortola is saying, "What is a traffic light?" (The other half is too young to drive.) I tried to explain the traffic light to my friend the other day. I have traveled around the Western hemisphere a good bit, and so I do know what traffic lights are.

I told him, "A traffic light is a stick at the intersection with three lights on it. One is red, one is orange, and one is green. When the red light is lit up, you stop. When the green is lit up, you go. When the orange is lit up, you stop if you can, or go if you can't."

My friend wrinkled up his forehead and stared at me to see if I was making a joke. Then he sucked his teeth loudly and muttered, "Cheese and bread! THAT will NEVER work!"

And I have to agree.

Tortolians are a friendly lot and prefer speaking in person rather than over that newfangled phone system that requires you dial all seven numbers now instead of the usual five numbers. So at a red light, folks will seize the opportunity to chat with their neighbors in other cars and totally ignore the red-yellow-green lights. When they are through chatting, they will have forgotten why they stopped in the first place, and simply hit the gas and go forward, whether the light is red, yellow, or green.

Furthermore, many pedestrians use this intersection, and there is no provision for them. So they too will merrily ignore the lights and cross the road when they please, because they know that everyone on Tortola will stop for a pedestrian in the road anyhow.

Then there are the cows. Yes, the cows. This particular intersection has a roving herd of cattle. They often walk down the grassy median, munching their way to town and back. However, since palm trees were recently planted in the median (the auto-body shops wanted more work, and trees in the median seemed like a good idea). Anyhow, the cows now have to wander out into traffic to get around the palm trees, and the cows do not care what color the traffic light is!

And then we have the drag racers that use that road at night for their pleasure. They have decided that since the traffic lights have a sequence of green-yellow-red, they will line up for the start of the race on the green light. Then when it turns yellow, they rev their engines up. When the light turns red, it's the signal for the race to begin! Varoooooom! They are off to a night of drag racing.

"What's a traffic light?" is bound to be asked all over Tortola for next few years.

Just like when we got fax machines. The rest of you (who live anywhere but Tortola) were getting Internet access years ago, while at the same time that we were just beginning to get fax machines (Tortola being at least a decade behind the rest of the developed world). I had been using fax machines 10 years previously when I lived on the Mainland; so many fax questions were targeted at me.

What is fax? Is it like sex? Wanna fax with me
wink *wink*?

Can I have safe fax?

Do I need anyone to fax with or can I fax alone?

Is it okay to fax in a group?

Will fax be served in the bars now?

Will fax be available at happy hour prices?

Will fax only be served on the fool moon parties?

Should I keep my faxing a secret or is it okay if my wife knows?

Can I fax with just anyone or only just friends?

What do I tell the kids about fax? And at what age?

Should I warn them about adult faxers?

Can I get a disease from faxing with strangers?

You gotta laugh, at the madness, of living in paradise; where craziness is the norm and sanity is rarely tolerated. If you don't laugh, you won't be happy with da way t'ings run. Don't worry, be happy.

As The Anchor Drags...
(News from the nautical soap opera)
Two Ladies On The Internet

Author's note: The following conversation took place over the Internet. Names have been changed to protect the guilty.

For those of you not familiar with the shorthand of on-line conversations, I offer these interpretations, as used in the following text:

ROFLMAO = Rolling On Floor Laughing My A** Off
ROFLMPO = Rolling on Floor Laughing My Panties Off

Miss Dolly: Aaarrrrrrrrrrggggggggghhhhhhhhhh! Matey!

ZEA ROZE: Howdy pardner!

Miss Dolly: What are you doing?

ZEA ROZE: Cursing the AOL

Miss Dolly: So, cursing AOL?

ZEA ROZE: Yeah. Oh, I mean cruising! I am at 2400 baud. Ugh! *So slow!*

Miss Dolly: Went sailing last Thursday. And went *SPLASH* in the drink! Fell off the frigging dock!

ZEA ROZE: Not again!!!!!!!!!!!!!!!!!!

Miss Dolly: Literally! That's not all...

ZEA ROZE: Funny, I suggested for the soap opera, "As The Anchor Drags," that a jealous wheelbarrow ran you off the dock... Had NO idea you had really fallen off!

Miss Dolly: Didn't bring any extra clothes because I figured.... well, it's alpha... I won't get wet.... So, putting the boat away (heavy...48') had the bowline and was leaning into it (like, windsurfing) using all my weight. (What little weight I have against this beast!) Apparently the bowline had been caught on something. All of a sudden, had more line than anticipated. And *splash*! Into the water! My friend said, "All I saw were your little Doc Martens going under..."

ZEA ROZE: Oh NOoooooooooooooooooooooooo oooooo

Miss Dolly: So, he grabs me up out of the water and pulls me up on the dock. Then brings me down below. Pulls my clothes off and throws me in the shower.

ZEA ROZE: And…? (Can we talk about this on AOL? Sounds a bit steamy!)

Miss Dolly: So, I get some of his clothes only he is a *tad* larger than me. I put his pants on and *whooosh* they go straight to the floor. Had to use a bit of line to hold them up! He loaned me a T-shirt too, but a bit tight on me, if you know what I mean. There is a dryer in the men's locker room…

ZEA ROZE: So you go in the men's locker room dressed as a man and dry your clothes!

Miss Dolly: Not the way I filled out his T-shirt, they'd know right away I wasn't a guy!

ZEA ROZE: ROFLMPO!

Miss Dolly: Rick put my pants and top in the dryer for me, but I was too embarrassed to give him my undies. I put my lacy bra and panties in a little plastic bag, you know, the kind you get from a grocery shop, has little handles. So anyway, obviously I go straight to the bar to wait on him to wash and dry my clothes. And there are hooks under the bar for women's purses....

ZEA ROZE: Yeah, that's a handy thing they have there.

Miss Dolly: So I hooked my plastic bag under there with my new Victoria's Secret undies in it soaking wet. Rick eventually came back with my dry clothes and said I could return his later (the one's I had borrowed and was wearing). I had a few drinks and left, got home, and then realized I had left my wet undies hanging on the hook at the bar!

ZEA ROZE: NO! Did you really? With all those blue blazers there? You left your undies at the bar?

Miss Dolly: Can you imagine....

ZEA ROZE: Oh now that is just GREAT!

Miss Dolly: Yep, right there at the Yacht Club.

ZEA ROZE: So, call them up and go get them!

Miss Dolly: What? And tell them I left my unmentionables at the bar the other night? ROFL-MAO!

ZEA ROZE: The WET ones... from Victoria's Secret Catalog!

Miss Dolly: I ain't gonna never retrieve them! Nope! Not me, sister! Cuuuuuuute bra and panties, too! Brand new! Virgin run on the bra!

ZEA ROZE: Ooooooops!

Miss Dolly: Can you imagine! I am soooooo embarrassed!

ZEA ROZE: They still got the undies? Send a BIG man around to collect them for you.

Miss Dolly: No way... tee hee! If my boyfriend found out I left my undies at the bar, boy would I have some explaining to do.

ZEA ROZE: Just tell him the truth.

Miss Dolly: What? Tell him I went sailing with another guy while he was at work? NO way, babe!

ZEA ROZE: You want me to call the Yacht Club for you?

Miss Dolly: Okay, but DON'T tell them it was me!

ZEA ROZE: Okay, stand by, I'll call now and get back to you.

ZEA ROZE: Argh, matey! Your undies are famous! Came in second place!

Miss Dolly: What? You be jiving, chica! Whatcha mean, SECOND place?

ZEA ROZE: Seems last Saturday the Yacht Club hosted a model boat show and race for the kids. The kids build their own models and race them or show them. Some kids can't afford the remote controls, so they just build a model and display it for awards. Anyhow, one kid was short on funds and had no sails for his model boat. The bartender gave him YOUR undies as a joke. Told the kid to make something out of that! So the kid took your bra and rigged his cutter with the cups. And he used your panties as the main sail.

Miss Dolly: Noooooooooo!

ZEA ROZE: Yep, he put the boat on display and came in second place. Got a ribbon too! Everyone likes his sexy sails, plus the name of the boat—

Miss Dolly: My undies came in second place in a boat show? Oh now that's a gas! ROFLMPO!!! What did he name the boat?

ZEA ROZE: Name of the boat is "Pardon Miss Dolly!"

Miss Dolly: You've GOT to be kidding!

ZEA ROZE: Hey, go by the bar and check it out yourself. They told me the model boats are on display for another week.

A Letter To Mom From Grace Klutz

From Grace Klutz
Aboard the Frying Crowd
West Indies

Dear Mom,

Everyone seems to know me now in Cruz Bay. Yep, your infamous daughter is responsible for putting Bea behind bars. That was after I punched her out cold. The police apologized for bothering me and wished the rest of my stay to be pleasant.

Everywhere I go in town now, pure strangers walk up to me and shake my hand. I seemed to have met the whole island. Many have congratulated me; others giggle. I can't pay for a drink anywhere. Everyone wants to toast me.

Me? I am a tad bit embarrassed, not being used to all this attention. I heard Bea finally got out of jail and hasn't been seen much since. They say she has two huge black eyes. I only hit her once, mama, honest. She must outweigh me by fifty pounds. Oh, and I seem to have a new boyfriend, Bea's ex. So I am known as the woman who came to town, punched out Bea, had her thrown in jail, and then stole her boyfriend. Bea wasn't exactly all that popular, as you might gather, even though she had been living with a very popular, roving musician. I wasn't popular at all! This was only my third trip to Cruz Bay.

I'll start at the beginning. I am the purser on the tall ship, *Frying Crowd.* We're a 100+-year-old rust-bucket, hauling tourist cargo. The captain thought my situation riotously funny. I felt I had to tell him before he heard the rumors. The coconut telegraph has amazing speed. He sort of is responsible for what happened. He, after all, sent me ashore in Cruz Bay to start with. See, at dinner, I dine with the captain, since we are both single and it looks good for the tourists. He told me to go ashore on the first launch after dinner and check out all of Cruz Bay's entertainment possibilities for Wednesdays and Sunday evenings, since our ship stops overnight on those days. I have to clear us all in and out of customs and immigration since we are foreign flagged with foreign crew in foreign waters. Isn't that a mouthful!

Well, mama, you know how I like music. So I was thrilled to go out on the town in search of live entertainment. I ended up at the Crow's Nest Bar. It is on the third floor of a waterfront building, with a gorgeous view of the harbor and my ship anchored out. A lovely band called the

Bailin' Whalers plays there on Sunday nights. I sat at the bar, listening to the band and chatting with the bartender. He refused to let me pay for any drinks, at the prospect of me continuing to bring a shipload of people to his bar every Sunday and Wednesday evening for libations and music.

When the Bailin' Whalers went on break, the mandolin player came up to the bar for a drink. I complimented him and the band, promising to bring my passengers and crew the next week. We chatted quite amicably. I could tell he was interested, flirting and all with me. When the band finished around 11:30 p.m., he took me to the Backyard Bar where we had a few drinks and talked until the last launch took me back to the ship at 1 a.m. I told him I would be back on Wednesday, and he asked if I could meet him for dinner.

Wednesday rolled around, and I cleared our ship through customs and immigration in my starched white uniform with gold bars. Then I strolled through the town's little park to the Central café, which is in a garden type setting at the edge of the park. My date, Jules, was sitting at a large round table with several of his friends. They were duly impressed by my uniform and bars, making a big show of dusting and wiping out the chair before I sat down.

Jules introduced me to the people scattered around the cafe. He seemed to know everyone there. I told him I had to catch the next launch back to the ship and finish my work. Then I would come ashore again in my regular clothes. The captain doesn't want us out partying in our uniforms in public. Now many folks proudly strut around in their yacht uniforms day and night whether on or off duty. Not us. The captain said crews on ships had ways of having too much fun, and perhaps it was better to be wearing street clothes rather than ship's clothes, should one do something a bit untoward. Like the chef who got so drunk ashore in her uniform that good Samaritans threw her into a dinghy and escorted her out to her boat. Left her passed out drunk in the cockpit.

She worked aboard a 180-foot ketch named *Gypsy*, a popular boat name in these parts. The boat she was dumped on by her good Samaritans was also named *Gypsy*, but it was a 34-foot vessel owned by a sweet little man who hadn't been with a woman in ages. He was ashore partying and when he grew tired, he decided to go home to his boat and feed his cat, Wendy. He had a few drinks tucked in his belly.

So imagine how surprised and pleased he was to find a 20-something pretty woman passed out in his cockpit. He had met her ashore. Because she was wearing her uniform t-shirt that said *Gypsy*, he had remarked to her that his boat was named *Gypsy*. She was polite but had dismissed him. He could tell. Her eyes kept roving while he was talking to her, as if she were thinking, "Why is this old man of 42 eyeballing me, when I am only 20-something." So he let her slip away and flirt the night away.

Now here she was in the cockpit. Asleep. He chatted to her, and she continued to sleep. So he decided that she would be more comfortable naked. He undressed her, and still she slept.

Well, heck, it had been a very long time since the little man had been with a woman. Nine months of cruising the islands and only meeting other couples cruising around, single men cruising around, and very few available women he felt like striking up a relationship with long enough to sleep with them.

So he took advantage and made love to her while she slept. Afterwards, he sat in the cockpit drinking a rum and coke, staring at the sleeping woman. Suddenly her mouth fell open and she started snoring like a lumberman's chain saw that needed a muffler and couldn't stay running so had to be loudly restarted every half minute. The ruckus was unbearable.

Quickly he dressed the young woman, tossed her into his dinghy and drove her out to her 180-foot sailboat. A young bemused deckhand came out and helped scooped the still sleeping woman on board. As the little man drove away, he could see the deckhand scratching his head and staring at the drunken chef passed out on the deck.

A few weeks later, she got an awful morning sickness that just wouldn't go away. This is a very bad thing for a yacht chef to have under any circumstance. The captain gave her a leave of absence to get well. I had run into the captain and he told me she was pregnant and was telling everyone that it's not hers, as she didn't sleep with anybody. He said that her mother was flying in with a straight jacket to take her home. Or somewhere.

And so I was hired to take her place for a while. But suffice it to say our captain strongly urged us not to wear our uniforms when we were clearly off duty.

I heard her story in two parts. The first part I heard from the captain about how the deckhand received her from a dinghy named *HoBo* late at night and the part where she went crazy because she was pregnant and swore it wasn't hers.

About a year later I met a nice little man on a boat named *Gypsy*. He was so nice I dated him for months. One night to entertain ourselves after dinner, we sat on the beach telling silly stories. He happened to mention that he had repainted his dinghy and failed to repaint her name back on her. He said the very next morning he was going to paint *HoBo*. My jaw fell open.

I asked him if he had any children and he looked at me oddly, as we had been through this stage months ago on our first date. We were each divorced, with no children. He replied, "None! Well, none I know of!" and gave me a wink.

When I announced he has one now, his jaw dropped and he eyed my belly and his eyes grew wide with horror. I quickly added, "It's not me! I can't get pregnant!" And I told him, oh man; this reminds me of Paul Harvey on the radio. So imagine Paul Harvey's voice as you read this

And now, here's the rest of the story.…

I told him all about the chef I had been filling in for while she went to get her head examined and what have you. And how the captain always said it was fitting that the chef came home drunk in a dinghy named *HoBo* with a strange little man.

I eyeballed my 42 year-old petite date with long wild dirty blond curls flying in the breeze and his big round eyes. He bursts out laughing and announces he is having another drink.

About three drinks later, he tells me *the rest of the story (thank you Paul Harvey for announcing that!)*.

He swears he had never done that before, but he had never come home to a young drunk pretty thing like that draped in his cockpit at 2 a.m. either. The next morning over coffee he claimed that he made it all up. So I pretended to believe him. But honestly, how many boats named *Gypsy* have a little man with a dinghy named *HoBo*.

Oh mama, the things you learn, the stories you hear, when you travel at sea like I do.

Anyway, back to my story about Jules and Bea. After Jules introduced me in the café, I noticed some raised eyebrows around the table, but figured it was just curiosity because I was new in town. I came into shore later, and mama, we had a splendid time. He is such a nice gentleman. I let him know that the following Sunday our ship would return there, and he let me know he would be playing music. So he asked if perhaps I'd have a date with him after he finished his performance.

Sunday rolled around, and I had to go ashore during the day to do my customs and immigration clearances. While strolling back to the dock, a strange fat woman snuck up behind me and swats my derrière! Can you imagine? I looked at her as she skipped away from me, and she looked sort of pathetic. I figured she was high on some sort of drugs, or drunk, or both.

Later when I came ashore, this crazy gal snuck up on me again and slapped me really hard on the back. I turned and ran, figuring she was going to mug me. It didn't occur to me to mention it to Jules. He was playing music most of the night, and then we went to the Treehouse for drinks. That demented woman crept up behind me and hit me again.

The place was rowdy, crowded, and noisy. I turned to Jules (we were still standing in a line of sorts at the bar waiting to get drinks) and said, "Did you see that?"

"See what?"

"That crazy crackbrain that hit me!"

"Crackbrain?"

"Some crazy woman who looks high on something bad has been sneaking up on me and slapping me on the back. That's the third time today."

"No, I didn't see that. How weird! Well, welcome to Cruz Bay, the world's largest open-air insane asylum."

We didn't bother to discuss it further. Obviously, there seemed to be a lot of strange people in Cruz Bay. I'd just have to keep a careful eye out for this lunatic. I made it back to the ship without incident. The next Wednesday, Jules and I went out for dinner at a very nice Italian restaurant. Then we went out to his boat. I couldn't help but notice that it had a lot of female-type stuff on it. I guess he saw me looking at the evidence. He volunteered that he used to live with a girl, but she had moved off the boat. He was still waiting for her to get the rest of her things. I replied something profound, like, "Oh."

That was all that was said about that. You know how I am mama. Discussing my current amour's previous ex-lover is about as exciting to me as watching a jockstrap mildew.

The next Sunday, I went to the bar with a bunch of passengers to hear The Bailin' Whalers play. My guests were on the outer deck where the band was, and I was inside an alcove sitting at the bar talking to the dentist and the bartender. I was only drinking Ginger Ale, because I wanted to stay sober for Jules for when he got off work later. Then we would go have a drink somewhere.

Well, this lunatic came in the bar. I never saw her sneak up on me. I had my long dark hair plaited into a French braid. My back was to the only exit.

Suddenly, my hair is grabbed ferociously, my head is snapped back (you could hear my neck crack), and I spun around on my barstool to look face-to-face at this insane woman. She was blocking the path towards the exit. Behind me was a window, but we're on the third floor, so I thought that I shouldn't be diving out of windows quite that high. Mama, I lost my head, and swung at the woman with all my might while still sitting on the barstool. She toppled backwards and blacked out for a moment, spread-eagled on the floor. I eyeballed the exit for a hasty escape but the bartender startled me by clamoring over the bar and picking the woman up off the floor just as she came to, heaving drunken expletives. He literally dragged her against her will out of the bar and down the stairs. The manager came up the stairs, as he'd heard the loud thud. The bartender told him that he was expelling the woman for attacking his patron.

The band saw none of this, and thank goodness neither did any of the passengers. It all happened so fast. I was shook up really bad, the dentist couldn't stop laughing, and the bartender wanted to buy me a drink. I accepted another Ginger Ale, apologizing all the while. I told them that she had hit me before and that I didn't know who she was. Hitting her seemed the only alternative to jumping out of the window. It had been drilled into me at self-defense training classes to "STUN and RUN!"

Still, much to my embarrassment, the bartender and dentist thought the whole incident amusing. Then the manager came up the stairs and told me that the police wished to see me. He had put them in his office rather than allowed them in the bar. The manager knew I was purser of the ship in the harbor and that his bar would be nearly empty instead of overflowing were it not for my suggestion to the passengers that they should come to the Sea Dogs Bar to hear the Bailin' Whalers.

I walked as tall as I could to go meet the police. I am terrified of men with guns. I wondered what would happen to me. We went down the stairs, and I saw the disheveled woman sitting at a table. While rising out of her chair, she screamed, "That's the bitch that knocked me out!"

The cops grabbed her and told her to sit down and be quiet. I was not in my ship's uniform, as you know, but I was all dressed up for my later date. The manager escorted me and one of the policemen into his office, while the other cop guarded the loony woman.

I told the cop about this demented woman and that when she grabbed my hair, yanking my neck back, it shocked me into action. I apologized profusely, explaining I'd never hit anyone before, but that I had been to this self-defense course, and it just came at me to "stun and run." Only, I didn't run because the bartender graciously hauled my foe off.

The policeman wanted to know how I knew this woman and what our relationship was to each other. I explained that I hadn't a clue who she was and that I thought she was trying to mug me when she first attacked me.

I went on to say I was a ship's officer and so on. I stood close enough so that they could smell my breath and tell that I had had nary a drop of alcohol to drink. Meanwhile, the bartender came into the office. He duplicated virtually the same story.

Now the cops wanted to know if I wanted to press charges against the madwoman. I said, "No, not really. But I do wish she would quit harassing me. I don't even know who she is. I think she's on some kind of bad drugs."

The cops conferred for a few minutes, and then we all went out of the office. The dame was still sitting there in dirty shorts and an old t-shirt, with a baseball cap pulled rakishly to one side of her head. She started cussing at me, as I walked by ignoring her. The cops arrested her for disorderly drunken conduct or something like that, and hauled her off to jail.

I went back upstairs with the bartender, while the band played on. They never saw the cops either. Now, I decided that I would have a strong drink. The dentist told me I'd never have to buy another drink in that town again after word gets out. I told him that I hoped word never got out, as I was mortified and shaken.

The Bailin' Whalers took a break. Jules wandered over to the bar and gave me a hug and kiss. The dentist cracked up laughing. Jules looked at him strangely.

The dentist said, "She just walloped Bea and threw her in jail!"

Jules looked horrified. I start apologizing all over again, but he insisted on hearing the whole story. So I told him while the bartender agreed whole-wholeheartedly.

"You punched out Bea?" He gives me a look of incredulity.

"Is that her name? You know her? She's the one I told you about sneaking up and slapping me last week. Who is she?"

Here comes the drum roll, mama.

"Bea was my ex-girlfriend, the one who still has her junk on my boat."

"Oh. Oh, dear me!" I began looking around for a large dark rock to crawl under and hide.

Now, Jules started laughing heartily. The rest of the band gathered around and he told them what I have done. They thought it all so funny too. Apparently, the band had their own share of problems with Bea. To have her barred from the Sea Dogs Bar suited them just fine. I felt flustered and wanted to go back to the safety of my ship offshore. But Jules, said, "Why bother? After all, my and your troubles are firmly locked behind bars."

When he finished playing, we went out to his boat to visit rather than another tavern. I just didn't feel like being around other folks. He mentioned that perhaps he should pack up the rest of Bea's stuff and drop it off at the jail for her. I decided I should go home to my ship, and Jules took me out in his dinghy.

The next Wednesday, we went back into Cruz Bay. I did my clearances then headed for the post office. A strange woman came up to me. I tried to avoid her, but she stopped right in front of me.

"Are you Grace Klutz?"

I managed to stammer out an uncertain, "Yes."

"Well, I want to shake your hand. I like your style. You blow into Cruz Bay, pick up the most popular man in town, punch out his old girlfriend, throw her in jail, then just walk off with him, cool as a cucumber. Hi, my name is Lucy. I never could stand Bea, and she was very bad for Jules. Look, I want us to be friends because I don't want to *ever* get on your wrong side!"

She winked at me knowingly, pumping my hand.

Mama, Cruz Bay is the oddest place. I didn't know whether to be amused, flattered or mortified. It's been that way ever since, pure strangers coming up to me, sizing me up, and making odd remarks about this most unfortunate incident.

Jules and I never discuss Bea, but I noticed all of her stuff has disappeared from his boat now.

Love and hugs,
Grace

T'iefin' Teeth

Author's Note: In da islands, the "h" in words often remains silent, so thief is pronounced teef or t'ief. And when ya take what's not yours, it's called t'iefin'.

Jungle Jim came into town one day from a distant island. While he professed one history, quite another was rumored about. The coconut telegraph was working overtime, as usual.

Looking for a place to live, he bought the ugliest, most derelict boat in the harbor. As a joke, and as a gesture of neighborly goodwill mingled with concern for his safety, the harbor residents amassed a collection of duct tape. At Jumby's bar that night, they lavishly presented the bag of tape to Jungle Jim as a boat-warming gift. Lord knows the poor fellow needed all the duct tape he could get. The boat had a million leaks on the deck, fortuitously none below the water line. While most yachtsmen would have been insulted to receive a bag full of half-used duct tape rolls, Jungle Jim was quite impressed at the thoughtfulness of the gesture and thanked his benefactors immensely. Thus, friends were made all around in the harbor and bar. And Jungle Jim settled in as a new neighbor on his floating derelict.

Jungle Jim proved to be a hard worker and an equally hearty partier. As he began to make some cash at various construction jobs, he began acquiring a new after-hours wardrobe centered on the hippie-cum-pirate look. Once a boring-looking man in tattered shorts and ripped T-shirts, he now sported colorful elastic-waist pants in wild prints, turned up to just below the knee. Atop that was a blousy buccaneer shirt with sleeves rolled up and the front rakishly open to mid-chest. A bandana with a skull in the center capped his long hair. A big gold earring dangled from one ear, and he let his beard grow out. Modest Jesus Sandals graced his big feet while a necklace of puka shells dangled around his neck with an old coin attached in the center front.

Women found him altogether nice and friendly, as did most everyone else. But when Jungle Jim would grant you one of his huge smiles, it was enough to make you want to think of a demolition team gone bad. Quite frankly, his teeth were a jagged, rotten mess. Some whispered it was bad drugs; others said it was bad upbringing; and still others thought it must have been due to bad luck.

Oh, he had a mouth full of teeth, but no tooth was complete. All ended in irregular jigs and jags of various yellow, beige, and brown hues. He was a sweet fellow, but when he gave you that great big smile, it made you want to cringe and stare at the skull and crossbones on his forehead bandana. A dentist had told him years ago that for a few thousand dollars, he could fix him up with a pretty smile. But Jungle Jim had never been able to raise the necessary funds, preferring to spend his extra cash on rum and women.

Like many other modern day pirates before him, he worked for cash and failed to file a tax return. He did eventually get around to registering his boat after getting harassed numerous times by the port authorities. But, like others before him lurking in the islands, he never quite got around to filing or paying income taxes. He made his money in cash and he spent it in cash. He never was motivated enough to save any cash up, at least not nearly enough to consider fixing his teeth.

Then the hurricanes hit the island. Much of the harbor and most of the island was devastated. The federal government sent down FEMA to assist with grants and loans for the hurricane victims that had suffered losses. The Red Cross showed up to handout food, camp stoves, radios, flashlights, and clothing vouchers good at the local stores, as well as vouchers for emergency medical care. Jungle Jim had none of the required paperwork to qualify for any of the FEMA benefits, despite the fact he lost his precious boat and all his worldly goods in the hurricane, including much of his treasured wardrobe. FEMA wanted pesky things like tax returns, deeds of ownership, paycheck stubs, utility bills addressed to you at your address, and so on.

However, the Red Cross only required a person to demonstrate need to qualify for the various handouts and donations. They didn't bother with much paperwork. You just stood in line, stated your case, and answered various questions. You didn't need the briefcase load of paperwork that FEMA required.

Jungle Jim got in line at the Red Cross to get a clothing voucher. It would be good for his favorite store, the one that sold black bandannas with little white skulls and cross bones on them, the one with the nifty colorful island boy pants and blousy buccaneer shirts. As he stood in line, he dreamed about the purchases he would make that afternoon. Indeed the storeowner, Chum Charlie (so named for his predilection to sudden seasickness at the most inopportune times), had told him to go ask Red Cross for a certificate for clothes then come back. Chum Charlie would give Jungle Jim anything he wanted in the store for half price, doubling the value of his voucher.

When Jungle Jim finally made it to the head of the Red Cross line, he told the Red Cross lady about losing his boat and all his clothes. She was very sympathetic, handing him a sack full of groceries and a prepaid voucher to use for clothes at any store on the island. She asked him if there was anything else he needed, such as any emergency medical care. Jungle Jim said no and left, after thanking the lady profusely for the Red Cross's generosity in such a time of need. He left, happy to go shopping for a few new outfits. He checked the sack of groceries. It was filled with cans of various sizes and included beets, fruit juice, lima beans, corn, peaches, and one plain can that simply read "beef."

He skipped merrily down the street, anxious to pick out his new clothes. Chum Charlie was happy to see him, as he was, after all, a frequent customer in the past. Jungle Jim chatted with him while he selected a stack of items and headed for the dressing booth. Several minutes later Jungle Jim came from the dressing room resplendent in long colorful batik pants with elastic at the ankles and topped with a vest of many colors made from bits of cloth like a quilt. And of course, the coveted pirate bandanna.

Chum Charlie admired Jungle Jim's good taste while tallying up his purchases. He still had a few dollars left on his voucher, so he told Jungle Jim to pick out a few more bandannas. While Chum Charlie bagged up Jungle Jim's old clothes and the newly purchased ones, he handed Jungle Jim the scissors to cut off the tags, since he planned to wear the clothes out of the store.

Jungle Jim beamed broadly at the storeowner, who flinched a tad bit like so many others when Jungle Jim blessed them with one of his gruesome toothy smiles. There was no one else in the store at the moment, so the owner wasn't afraid that he would embarrass Jungle Jim when he said, "You know, Red Cross has that emergency medical aid. I wonder if they could fix your teeth. You're a fine fellow but would look so good with a new smile."

All the while Jungle Jim smiled broadly at him and laughed, agreeing that would indeed be nice if the good old Red Cross would do that.

"You should ask them!"

Jungle Jim giggled and smiled some more, "Yeah, maybe I will. See you at Jumby's. I'm going there now. It's happy hour and I got on my new threads to show off. Plus I got a date with Peggy Sue. She's my new sweetie. Well, if you call eating a bowl of soup and having a few rums a date, that's where I'm headed."

"Yeah, see you later Jungle Jim."

"Later, mon."

Down the street ambled a happy Jungle Jim in his new outfit. He stopped at the corner of town, where the four corners meet, where lots of people stop to talk and trade gossip or money or drugs, depending on the time of day and the characters milling about. He studied the outdoor bulletin board posted under the big oak tree. Normally it listed where all the live entertainment was, who had spare puppies to give away, where to get a massage or learn yoga, along with a few lost and found notices coupled with panicky pleas from a pet owner whose pet was missing in action.

But since the hurricane had blown away all the old notices, it now boasted post-hurricane information. FEMA had a list of options available, as did Red Cross, on official looking papers tacked up on the board. On another notice was the schedule of days the unemployment office would visit the tiny island. If you could prove you had been working legally, you might qualify for unemployment if you weren't already banging nails in a roof somewhere.

Coupled with the official government and Red Cross notices were desperate scribbled notes from people looking for a place to live, an all too common problem after the hurricanes. Many were homeless. Seems half the island had moved around, crowding into the few remaining operational homes and apartments.

Jungle Jim studied the listing under the Red Cross notice, "Emergency Medical Care." He thought again about what the storeowner had said.

A few cars and trucks drove by, some honking and hollering hellos to Jungle Jim. It was customary in the islands to honk at everyone you knew, so town was often a cacophony of beeps and honks and yelled greetings. You always holler at your friends when you drive by them, if not honk. Jungle Jim smiled and waved and then crossed the street, walking the few blocks to his favorite watering hole. Up the stairs he went. He walked proudly and stately over to the bartender.

"Hiya Jungle Jim. New clothes?"

"Yeah mon, these be my new Red Cross Clothes. You like 'em?"

"Jungle Jim, you look great! What can I get you to drink?"

"I'll have a rum and coke, please."

"Coming up."

"Hey, you seen Peggy Sue?"

"Yeah, she was just here. I think she's in back watching the movie. I just sold her a Heineken."

"Cool."

Jungle Jim picked up his drink from the bar and wandered to the back deck of the bar where several patrons lazed about watching a movie on the VCR. It was one of the few bars that had electricity and running water. Tumbling Ted was passed out on one of the benches, Peggy Sue was talking to Rolanda at a table in the corner, and Big Ben was stretched out in a chair reading a paperback book. Three construction workers were engrossed in the movie, still dressed in cut-off shorts splattered with paint topped with saw-dusty T-shirts. Their table was generously littered with empty beer bottles and overflowing ashtrays.

"Hey darling!" Peggy Sue spun around in her seat and smiled at Jungle Jim. He proffered his gap-toothed grin and bent down to kiss her. These two were a hot item now. Before, Jungle Jim could never seem to keep a girlfriend. He liked to kiss and be kissed but most women just found the lack of dental work a bit much and couldn't bring themselves to kiss him except under the cover of darkness and *then* only after far too many drinks. But Peggy Sue was different. She had seen through the hideous smile to the good man behind it.

After the hurricane, Peggy Sue's roommate had left the island on the first flight out. This left Peggy Sue in a considerable jam, as she could not even begin to afford half the rent, much less all of it. Post-hurricane is no time to be relocating, as so many people are homeless and looking for shelters. Demand for living space is high, and supply is limited or nil, so looking for a new, smaller, cheaper place wasn't really an option for Peggy Sue.

During the hurricane Jungle Jim had stayed in the bar drinking all night while his boat was smashed apart by the stormy seas and floated away in bits and pieces. All he had ever been able to find of his beloved wreck was one old roll of duct tape that had ironically washed up on the beach.

You may wonder how he knew that wet sticky roll of duct tape was his. Well, a few months earlier during the "duct tape party" all his friends had given him partially used rolls of duct tape for his derelict boat as home warming gifts. One benefactor had scribbled "Good Luck" on the inside roll of the duct tape. He had picked up the "Good Luck" roll of duct tape from the beach and carried it into Jumby's bar that day, proclaiming he had FINALLY found some wreckage of his boat. While many patrons laughed, others commiserated with him. That night, he met Peggy Sue.

She was distraught over losing her roommate. Tips at the restaurant were not so good these days, and she was worried about the upcoming rent. With so many people looking for apartments, surely her landlord would kick her out if the rent wasn't paid in full and on time. It was due at the end of the week.

Jungle Jim bought her a few drinks and talked with her, telling his tale of woe of buying and losing the boat. Sometime during the evening she asked Jungle Jim where he would be staying now that he had lost the boat. He supposed he'd be sleeping at the bar; he had nowhere to go, save sleeping in the graveyard where many still camped out. The police evidently didn't think to enforce curfew at the graveyard, but anyone caught sleeping on the beach was hauled off to jail for the night.

Peggy Sue invited Jungle Jim to stay on her couch. At some point between the sunset curfew that forced them to retreat to her tiny apartment and midnight, he ended up in Peggy Sue's bed rather than on her couch.

What was even better was that Peggy Sue kissed him passionately, the way he liked. Oh, he had not been kissed like that in a *very* long time. Jungle Jim did his best to do everything he could to please Peggy Sue during the long windless night.

The next morning, over coffee and beer at Jumby's (since Peggy Sue's apartment still had no electricity and no cooking gas), Jungle Jim offered to pay half her rent if he could stay on. Peggy Sue was ecstatic. So that's how Jungle Jim ended up with a new girlfriend. It was literally the talk of the town for a few days as word spread that Jungle Jim and Peggy Sue were not only seeing each other but also living together. Neither cared about all the gossip. There were so few secrets to be had on this tiny island anyhow. Besides, Jungle Jim was secretly proud to be the talk of the coconut telegraph about anything other than his old duct-taped derelict of a wreck that he so fondly referred to as a boat.

Long before the hurricanes wiped out most of the sailing fleet, Jungle Jim was in Jumby's one night when a day-charter sailboat captain tacked his new brochure up on the wall over the payphone. The other captains, not to be outdone, eventually tacked their charter brochures on the wall as well. Soon the wall was nearly covered with colorful pictures of people sailing and drinking, dogs sailing with bandannas on their necks, and scores of idyllic beaches. Each one encouraged you to sail with them for the *ultimate* experience… and the parting of a hundred dollars per couple.

So Jungle Jim decided not to be outdone. He borrowed a Polaroid instant-print camera and forked over an outrageous amount for a pack of film. Back in the harbor he used up both packs taking pictures of his boat inside and out. Then he tacked these on the wall next to all the charter yacht brochures. The first showed the outside of his derelict boat, complete with sun-ripened, torn duct-tape hanging off the port side of the deck and dangling alongside chipped paint. He labeled the picture at the bottom of the white frame: "Charter the Derelict!"

The second snapshot showed the cockpit, replete with paint peeling off the seats and the tiller flaked in "solar-stripped" varnish. A lone cushion, lay on the seat, faded and ripped at the seams. The accompanying caption said: "Enjoy Derelict's Roomy Cockpit."

The third picture had a caption that read: "Gourmet Meals From My Galley." It showed a rusty camp stove with a small propane canister lying on the counter servicing it. Dirty coffee cups and empty beer cans littered the counter, as did wadded up cracker wrappers. A beat up cooler lay in the sole (floor) of the boat. If you studied the photo closely, you noticed that the edge of the galley counter had an unwrapped condom package on it.

The fourth scene was the interior salon of the boat. It showed bare foam rubber mattress with a wadded up, stained sheet tossed across it. The floorboards were warped plywood, and the portholes were dusted over in a grayish haze of dirt and cigarette smoke. Penned at the bottom of that picture in neat print was: "Your Luxurious Cabin."

The next one showed a bucket of seawater on the stern of the boat along with a solar shower bag and spout. It said: "Our Modern Head [bathroom] For Your Comfort."

As the fitting final photo, someone had taken a picture of smiling, gap-toothed Jungle Jim in his best pirate outfit, standing at the helm holding the tiller. That shot was plainly labeled: "Your Captain."

Big Ben, owner of the bar, thought the pictures hilarious when Jim proffered them up and insisted he staple then on the wall next to all the pretty charter boat brochures. For years Big Ben refused to remove them, even when the other captains complained. As the glossy charter brochures faded, their owners or captains would hastily tack up new glossy brochures. And Jungle's Jim's pictures stayed firmly in place, withering with the weather.

When tourists came into the bar and hee-hawed at the pictures, Jungle Jim would approach them and ask them in his most serious tone if they wanted to go sailing with him on Derelict. This was usually met by nervous giggles. So Jungle Jim in his affable way would steer them to one of the other captains and seal a charter deal for them. The grateful captains would buy Jungle Jim drinks in return. They offered him commissions, but he refused to accept them. He'd embarrass the captains by saying, "But we be neighbors, friends, and old salts, Matey!" A free drink or two was a good enough reward for Jungle Jim.

That night as Jungle Jim sat down, Peggy Sue admired his new outfit, courtesy of the Red Cross voucher. He called her "little darling," thanked her, and leaned over to give her another kiss. They spent a fun evening with their friends in the bar, eating and drinking. Around ten o'clock they left arm in arm to walk up the hill to the tiny apartment they now shared.

Jungle Jim hung up his new purchases in the closet by candlelight, telling Peggy Sue he wished he could figure out a way to get some of that Red Cross emergency medical money to fix his teeth. But how to prove they were a result of hurricane damage and not the result of lifelong neglect and prior drug use?

Peggy Sue kicked the idea around in her head. She came up with a plan. Tomorrow she would go shopping before work, and then she and Jungle Jim would go to work. Afterwards they would meet at Jumby's Bar.

The next day she stopped by the drug store. She bought some denture adhesive, a box of Chiclets chewing gum (the nice, neat, square white gum that comes in a little box), and a cardboard camera that had 12 exposures and a built in flash. Throughout her day at work, she prayed her scheme would work. She liked Jungle Jim immensely, but heaven forbid that hideous grin did make her wince.

That afternoon at Jumby's, Peggy Sue reviewed her plan with Jungle Jim. He roared with laughter, startling Big Ben from behind the paperback he was engrossed in. The bartender looked over hopefully, as if it might have been a good joke he missed. Other than Tumbling Ted snoozing in the corner, the place was nearly deserted. It was still early, before many had gotten off work yet.

Peggy Sue and Jungle Jim slipped into the sole restroom in the place. It was painted dark blue with stellar constellations on the ceiling. A large mirror with an immense bamboo frame hung over the sink. Peggy Sue applied the denture adhesive to the gum, carefully placing one on the front of Jungle Jim's jagged upper tooth. He glanced in the mirror and roared with laughter.

"Be still! We've got a few more to go," said Peggy Sue as she began to apply adhesive to three more Chiclets. Through a haze of giggles, she managed to finally get them more or less applied to Jungle Jim's teeth. It took a bit of arranging and Jungle Jim had to peel his lips back, appearing grotesque as she worked.

"Don't move, let the adhesive set." Sue admonished him as he stood there looking frightfully ridiculous.

Jungle Jim tried to be still, but he just had to turn and look in the mirror. He laughed as Peggy Sue shushed him.

Meanwhile, people were starting to amble into the bar after their day's toil on the island. Many were weary construction workers in dirty jeans and smelly t-shirts. They would glance at the restroom as laughter and giggles erupted from behind the closed door. The bartender shrugged his shoulders.

"Jungle Jim and Peggy Sue, acting like they're having their honeymoon in Jumby's restroom," he said with a wink and a knowing look. The workers ordered beers as they left the couple alone to giggle and laugh. Bushes outside that needed watering could be pressed into service if the couple hogged the restroom any longer.

Inside the restroom, Peggy Sue intoned, "Practice your smile."

Jungle Jim stared at the mirror and tried to smile without cracking up entirely and blowing the scene. Eventually he got the hang of holding his mouth just so, trying to resemble a healthy, toothy smile. The ensuing pictures would be not-so-clear close-ups anyway, as it was a disposable cheap camera after all.

Outside in the bar, Otis speculated obscenely about what the couple in the restroom might be doing, much to the laughter of all. Then suddenly the door opened, and all twelve patrons lined up on various bar stools turned to look at Jungle Jim and Peggy Sue emerging. Jungle Jim was holding his mouth a funny way, and my goodness he had teeth! BIG teeth!

Parrot Petey hollered, "My God, Jungle Jim! You have teeth!"

But Jungle Jim could not control himself and broke into his usual beamy smile, which revealed the Chiclets gum along with his usual hideous yellow, brown, and black jagged teeth showing on the sides. Lefty Louie had just taken a swig of his beer, which he now spewed out across the bar and erupted in choking laughter. Parrot Petey slapped him on the back. This was rewarded with a healthy burp from Lefty Louie and laughter from others.

With the cheap camera, Jungle Jim's friends spent the afternoon photographing him cavorting around with his girlfriend and other friends. They were all in on the scam. Everyone wanted to see him get his teeth fixed. No one thought it would really happen. All the pictures were happy ones, with his friends howling with laughter every time the Chiclets chewing gum smile flashed.

After exhausting the roll of film about the same time the gum starting dissolving and making a royal mess, Peggy Sue dashed off to turn it in for next-day processing. The photographer's shop had a generator; so many folks were bringing in rolls of film to document their house damage for recalcitrant insurance companies and FEMA promises. The young couple anxiously awaited development of the pictures while downing copious amounts of beer.

The next day they picked up the pictures and some looked downright ridiculous. But some looked incredibly real as Jungle Jim flashed his Chiclets chewing gum grin at the camera. Holding his mouth and lips just so, it actually looked almost believable. Several friends were in the picture with him, so they surmised that if push came to shove, they could prove they knew him when he had great teeth.

The next day, after fortifying his courage with two beers, Jungle Jim went to the Red Cross. The Red Cross worker flinched when he gave her his cracked brown and yellow-toothed smile.

"I need help with emergency dental care," he said in a low, sweet voice as he pulled out the pictures of his smiling Chiclets chewing gum face.

"You see, I was staying at the bar during the hurricane, because it wasn't safe to be on my Deril—um, boat and one of the storm shutters came loose at the bar. So I went outside to try to put the shutter back on, and all of a sudden this huge coconut flew at me, and hit me in the mouth, knocking out some of my teeth and chipping all the rest."

Then he gave her his best chipped-tooth smile. She winced and tried to smile back at him.

She gave his explanation some thought and then looked at him skeptically.

She was old, she was tired, and it was sad listening to everyone's tale of woe all day long. My, he did have a mess in his mouth. She looked at the picture, and she looked back at him.

"Who is your dentist?"

Oh, how thankful he was for his girlfriend rehearsing him the night before.

"I don't have one. I mean I did, back in the states, but when I came here, my teeth were in such great shape, I never needed a dentist. I was going to get them cleaned, but then the hurricane came and knocked most of them out, so it seemed pointless.

"Okay, who was your dentist in the states?"

"Oh, that was Doc Brown in Fort Lauderdale, but he died three years ago at the age of eighty-four. I wouldn't know where my dental records are now. That's why I brought you these pictures of my Chic... I mean smiles... smiles of me with my chick! Yeah that's it."

The Red Cross worker looked at the pictures again and let out a long, slow sigh. She was tired, but it was her duty to help. She slowly began filling out the forms. She wasn't sure about this; something told her that something was off here, but the young man was so nice. Those pictures didn't seem quite right, but she couldn't place a finger on it. Oh well, it was her chance to help somebody out, and the dentist probably needed the business so she handed him the completed voucher.

The next day he eagerly dashed into the town's dentist and asked him to fix his teeth, handing him the voucher from the Red Cross to pay for it. The dentist wanted to know how he qualified, as he knew the young man had always had bad teeth; he'd seen him around town before.

"Don't ask. Just fix them, *please!* Purdy please? The voucher is good. Won't ya help me Doc?"

The dentist pondered and thought about how business had been terribly off since the hurricane. People weren't keeping their appointments, and most had no money for dental work. He thought of the rent coming due next week from his unpleasant landlord. He smiled at the young man.

"Have a seat, let's take a look here. Hmm. What's this stuff stuck to your front teeth? It looks like denture grip!"

"No Doc, that's just some bad mashed taters that stuck there…."

Within a few weeks, Jungle Jim was dancing in his steps, giving everyone his usual large smile; only this time he received numerous compliments on the "new look."

A few weeks later, two happy people with gorgeous smiles trotted down the aisle for

marriage, dressed as colorfully as they could muster in their modern-day retro-pirate clothes.

A happy ending for all? I guess so.

Da-Fema-Mon!

Prologue...

Hurricanes Luis and Marilyn slammed into the U.S. Virgin Islands in September of 1995, just ten days apart. The damage to the islands was substantial, and the tourist economy was wrecked. The federal government, always quick to meddle into ordinary lives, sent down their FEMA team, a government agency. I think FEMA stands for Federal Emergency Management Act, but it could be renamed Free Easy Money for All.

FEMA has this wonderful program to give out lots of grants and loans, and some of the money ends up with people who do not deserve it or lie and cheat to get it. This is what happens when you give away money at the speed and magnitude that FEMA does. Those who could not qualify for loans were often handed outright grants. It was specified that this money should be used for the hurricane damages. The recipients were sometimes creative in spending for their indemnifications. Others simply dropped their grant into various struggling bars. Quite a few ran out to buy a new car. That way they could travel *in style* around the island, gawking at the hurricane damages.

One unique aspect about the islanders is that their tendency towards piracy never quite vanished. Such was the attitude of these initial easy grants. Oh sure, some people actually did use theirs to replace their roof. Many enjoyed the sudden wealth as a vacation spree, money to blow for fun. To heck with the hurricane damages—pass the rum.

While some people qualified for free grants, others were eligible for loans at four-percent interest, for up to thirty-years. The good ole federal government had a law that no one could be discriminated against because of *age*. Thus people in their eighties discovered they could get a thirty-year loan to buy a boat or home. This was where common sense clearly sailed out to sea on a leaky vessel.

While it sounds all neat and charitable for the federal government to offer all this aid, in reality, I think it hurts more than helps. But then, nobody asked me. As the government made the pronouncements about people qualifying for disaster unemployment benefits and businesses able to get low interest loans, some decided it was more economical to stay *out* of business than to reopen for the season.

It would have been nice if FEMA had hired help locally, rather than sending all their statesiders in. Those people had never been to this area before and had no clue as to the culture shock they would experience. This isn't Kansas, Toto. Even if they had landed before the hurricane, they still would have found themselves bewildered.

Take St John for instance. A beautiful island, part of the U.S. territory, famous for it fifty-plus beaches and National Park. It is a unique place with an eclectic mixture of people, some *born-heres* (pronounced locally *bonn-hair*) with a long lineage to prove their native status. Others were recent transplants from all over the world, but most were from the U.S. Some don't want to admit where they are from, since they are considered *persona-non-gratis* in a few faraway places they don't care to remember.

In the sixties a bunch of hippies discovered cheap land on "the rock" as locals often call the place at times. It seemed like utopia. As St John surged in popularity, many others discovered the place too. Now some of these old hippies find themselves land-rich and loving it. On this island of colorful people and lifestyles, neither tie-dye nor the peace symbol ever went out of style. St John is where misfits are tolerated, oddity accepted, and individuality embraced.

The island grew faster than her infrastructure. Population expanded at such a rapid rate that the phone company and post office could not keep pace. A whole new business sprang up—a private mail service where you, along with everyone else that joined, were issued the identical post office box number. This mail service would sort the mail. Customers collected it from the mail service's office, a block away from the U.S. post office. Then the mail service added a phone answering service because many people could not get phone service to their homes or they were home so rarely that there was no need for a phone.

Imagine a few thousand people with identical mailing addresses *and* identical phone numbers... Those who could not afford the mail service used General Delivery as their address, which meant their mail along with hundreds of others was held at the post office front desk. They would have preferred a post office box, but none were available. The post office was having trouble getting federal funds to expand. Their census figures did not agree with the tremendous volume the tiny post office endured. Plus they probably received more packages than any other post office serving a community of that size. Islanders like to mail-order their stuff. Shopping for ordinary things is severely limited on the island.

Social life on St John tends to be more in town at pubs, restaurants or parks, so there just didn't seem to be much need to put up street numbers or signs. When telling someone where they lived, people referred to the area such as Monte Bay, Bordeaux, or Gift Hill. At one point the Feds sent down money for road numbers. Suddenly St John began sporting signs saying Route 10 and Route 20. The locals never refer to the roads by the numbers. So if a tourist should ask if Route 10 goes to Crystal Bay, they are likely to get a shrug of the shoulders.

Another unique St John trait is most folks are on a first-name only basis with each other. To prevent confusion of similarly named people such as Bob, nicknames are bestowed upon them to distinguish them from others. So for example, there are three Bobs but one is called Baltimore Bob, another is known as BoBo, and the third is RoRo-Bob (because his boat was named RoRo).

Another little curiosity about the island is mode of transportation. Many do not have cars, nor do they want them. Hitchhiking is safe and acceptable. There are plenty of tourist taxis around frequenting the beaches. So getting around the island without a car is not really considered a hardship except on a dark rainy night.

The polite FEMA workers knew nothing about this wacky island lifestyle before they arrived.

One day, I interviewed a FEMA man. In his late sixties, retired, he had somehow ended up on contract to FEMA as standby help. In the states he had his own camper trailer. He drove to the various stateside disaster sites. This way, he had his own place to stay and didn't occupy much needed local housing after a disaster. When FEMA called him this time, they put him on a plane, then a taxi, then a ferry ultimately plunking him down on St John. He hadn't a clue where he was. He found the island's eclectic residents friendly but perplexing.

The rest of this story was told to me by *Da-fema-mon*, as the island residents affectionately renamed him. He was really another Pete, but the island already had a Pete, Peter, Petey, Pete-the-welder, Peter Pan (who was gay but didn't care about his nickname), plus PP, and a Peetsie. So someone named him *Da-fema-mon* to save us all from another variation on Pete.

Da-fema-mon and I were sitting in an open-air bar, where his office was now temporarily located. He was enjoying a cold beer. The story was periodically interrupted as he saw one of his cases walk down the street. He'd jump up, chase them down to get a piece of information for their file, or set up an appointment to visit their damages. Naturally, all the names and places have been changed to protect the innocent, guilty, and/or crazy.

Now let's let *Da-fema-mon* tell his story:

I'm on contract, and this is terrible because I hardly get any work done. People are late for everything. Most don't know where they live. You ask them for a street address. They say something like, "I live in Calabash Boom." I ask where that is and they say, "You know past the Tamarind tree in Crystal Bay, you take the second dirt road, or is it the third, let's see, oh, yeah, there are four graves there, turn at the four graves, anyhow, usually a bunch of goats are around there, and then you go past the sugar mill ruins, and then I'm like the third or fourth driveway on the left, the house with no roof."

Or they tell me they don't *know* where they live, and they say something like, "I rent from Mrs. Mudrakers at her place, you know, on top of the hill, near Jacob's Ladder, you know, past the tennis courts, that monstrous hill you have to drive over to get to the Hiyarent Hotel, her place is at the top, and I live on the first floor, the one with the east wall blown away."

They don't know the street name or the number of the house. Even the people with numbers in their neighborhood, the addresses make no rhyme or reason. They say something like "I live at 37-4221 Winding Estates." I get there (I think), but the numbers aren't even marked. If I'm lucky enough to ever find the neighborhood. I get lost sometimes, but I think I must be near the right place. So I get out and start asking neighbors for John Smith. I learn that instead of knocking on the door, you stand there and yell, "Inside!"

They answer back, I ask about John Smith, and they invariably say, "Never heard of him."

After awhile I find out that they all do know John Smith, but he's the guy everyone calls Pops or something like that. Neighbors don't even know the last name of the people living next to them. With all the nicknames these islanders seem to bestow on each other so as not to have to deal with last names, it is darn right confusing. The mail hardly delivers to any of the neighborhoods, so you can't rely on labeled mailboxes either. The streets don't seem to have names posted. Of course all of this could have blown away in the hurricane, but given the way that people don't seem to know *where* they live, is interesting to say the least. I wish now, I was getting paid *hourly* instead of under contract. It takes me twice the time to do half the work.

Let me tell you, the *new* FEMA forms should have a space that says, *"What do people call you?"* I mean, how I am I suppose to know that Robert G. Hill is really Baltimore Bob or that a woman who is named Candice R. Jones is actually called C-R.

One day, I picked up a new file, tracing the 12 Kingdomcome Street address to a bar. Funny, I figured no one would actually live in a bar; must be where they work. So I go in, and the place is full of people that seem very friendly. I ask for a William Bernard. By now, I was inured against anything. If somebody listed a bar as their address, then I'd just check right into it. Besides, if all else fails, I could have a drink. Funny, I never drank at all in the states. Here, I go out for breakfast; you know I get a per diem. There I am ordering eggs and bacon next to someone guzzling a few beers *before* work. Same at lunch. Simply amazing, the drinking habits down here!

I had tried calling William by phone for his appointment a few times. The phone number listed on the application turned out to be a bar payphone. No one who answered knew of him. So I go in person to try to find this guy and assess his damages.

I start with the bartender, and then asked ten or so patrons if they knew of William Bernard. Nobody knew. Last names are so rarely used on this small island, as if they can't be bothered with such detail.

A few good-natured drunks even laughed at the very idea that I was asking for someone by their last name. They immediately pegged me as the *Da-fema-mon*. Word spread that I was hopelessly trying to find someone by their *real* name!

In the very back of the bar, was another lower section, down a few steps, with tables, chairs, and a huge TV installed on a stage. One lone guy sat at an immense wooden table. He looked interesting enough, so I thought I might as well ask this character too and take some more comic abuse.

He was wearing a jaunty straw hat with a wide brim topped with a colorful hatband in tropical hues. His faded black t-shirt was immense, perhaps a quadruple X, managing to sort of drape across his large belly. Long dark hair rested on his shoulders, and a beard graced most of the front of the shirt. The club's logo was printed on a breast pocket.

"Howdy-do!" he smiled merrily as I approached him. "You must be Da-fema-mon."

I grinned, having long ago given up on introducing myself as Pete Perdu. The mere mention of one's last name could produce instant amnesia, if not laughter, in most islanders.

Sometimes I think I am just in a funny dream. I'll wake up back home in Kansas. A place where last names are known *and used*, a place where people know their own address *and* their phone number isn't a pay phone in a bar!

The other day, I called into headquarters to check on my messages. The receptionist asked my name, not recognizing my voice (probably cause I'd had a few beers.) You know, another day hanging around bars looking for my appointments to come staggering in any hour or two. Anyhow, she surely must have wondered what I was thinking when I told her I was *Da-fema-mon!* Boy, I was so embarrassed I just hung up on her.

So I smile back at the bearded man and say, "Yes, I'm Da-fema-mon. I'm looking for William Bernard."

"That's me!" he said as he smiled broadly, seeming to gush all over as if I'd just informed him I was Ed McMahon presenting his five-million-dollar sweepstakes check.

Without leaving his seat, he leaned over the table, sticking his hand out. I walked over and shook hands with him. That's when I saw the yellow post-it note stuck on the side of his hat. "My name is Beanie, please be nice to me" was neatly printed in pen. I wondered what kind of fruitcake I had stumbled into now.

"Here! Have a seat. What would you like to drink? Perhaps something to eat? We have a cook today. At least I think we do. Yo! Newfie! We got a cook today?" he shouted toward the bartender.

"Last I checked, Tofer was in there!"

A shaggy character was wiping his hands on a food stained apron as he walked out from behind the kitchen's swinging door. "Somebody call me?"

Next thing I know, Tofer is naming off the entire day's menu, which Beanie insists I order from while he's hollering at Newfie to get me a drink. You'd think I was the long awaited Messiah. Beanie told me the meal and drinks would be on the house. Then he thoughtfully added that there was a ladder in back if I needed it.

Funny, this guy owned the joint, yet none of his employees knew his real name. I tell you, this island is weird.

The beer was icy-cold, just like Beanie promised it would be. I sipped the proffered beer, thinking of the regulations I was breaking while drinking on the job. I must be getting dotty in my old age. I figured I better get this wrapped up while I was still sober. I went down the questions on my clipboard, first asking about his home address.

"Right here!" he beams.

"12 Kingdomcome Street?"

"Uh, maybe. Sounds right. I'd have to look it up in the phone book. That's what I did when I filled that out."

He pointed an enormous finger at my form. He began tossing stuff about, presumably looking for the phone book. From the looks of the massive table we sat at, he might indeed just live here. It had a collection of paperback books, three decks of cards, four ashtrays (all overflowing), several empty beer bottles, a few drained cocktail glasses, a stack of poker chips, two cigar boxes (one stuffed with copious tabs), half a pizza with dried-up anchovies on the side, a dirty t-shirt, a rotary file full of penciled in phone numbers, several colored pens, and a small child for all I could tell. She was curled up on the L-shaped built in bench table, next to Beanie, her back to us.

Long gorgeous red curls draped down her tiny back. I wondered what a child was doing sleeping in a bar in the middle of the day. She should have been in school, from the looks of her.

Later when she woke up and turned around I was quite startled to discover she was the town dwarf, a Little Person, thirty something years old and barely three feet tall. She had come to the island a few weeks ago. Rumor had it she was taking a break from a job at a strip tease joint in Miami. People said her stage name was *Sweet & Low.* You meet *all kinds* here, I'm telling you.

When I began asking Mr. Bernard various questions about his application, he got interrupted by all sorts of people who wanted to say hi or ask him a question. I noticed they all called him Beanie, so I penciled that under "other notes."

I noticed that every time someone would mention, "Okay, Beanie, I'll be nice to you," he would smile but look puzzled.

"Where do you sleep at night?" I asked Beanie.

"Oh, I got a room and a shower in the back. Want to see it?"

"Yeah."

He struggled up from his bench, the post-it note fluttered down to the table.

"What's this?" He picked it up and read it, then laughed out loud.

"Who put this note on my hat? Geez!"

He waddled over to the band stage, taking a step up, quite methodically. You could feel the vibrations in the floor as he walked. One of those people that just seems to walk heavily. Of course he had the bulk to give it some *real* heft.

He pulled back this huge American flag that was hanging as a backdrop across the stage, opened a door, and escorted me into his room. A single bed was built into the side of the wall. The rear-end of a big-screen TV was hanging from chains above, poking through the wall to face the audience in the bar. Built-in shelves on another wall all held plastic crates from an assortment of milk companies, all threatening penalties if used for any other purpose.

They contained an assortment of objects including a stack of bar t-shirts, more cigar boxes, several unopened bottles of shampoo and tooth paste, manila file folders crammed with papers, tin boxes with goodness knows what in them, plus packs and packs of pictures and negatives.

A small bar table beside the bed held an unsteady mountain of paperbacks, an empty soup bowl, some cleanly picked chicken bones, assorted silverware, three overflowing ash trays, and what looked like a marijuana cigarette stub. A bare light bulb dangled uncertainly from a nail on the wall. The mosquitoes were threatening to eat me alive. Beanie noticed my slapping and handed me a can of Ode-de-off.

"Oh, they are not nearly so bad today! Sometimes you can't even see in here for the little buggers."

He opened another door, which revealed a nicely tiled shower with a plastic curtain and a large beach towel draped over the curtain rod. To the left was a jug of bleach, and a bottle of baby powder sat on the floor next to a Nordic Walking track machine. Funny, I would have expected a commode and sink to be there. Straight ahead was another door, with kitchen type noises coming from behind it. I could smell my Reuben sandwich cooking.

Expansively spreading his hands out, Beanie eagerly declared, "This is home! I also have another bedroom behind the kitchen."

You would have thought he was showing me the Taj Mahal. I was thinking to myself, but the beer in me made me say it out loud, or maybe it was the heat, I don't know. But I blurted out, "This looks like a prison cell!" as I glanced at the windowless room with all its clutter and the Reuben odors competing with a stack of dirty laundry tossed in a corner. This didn't phase Beanie one bit.

"Yep! I got ten years to life, and been here five of them so far."

He flung open the next door, which took us into the eclectic kitchen. Tofer announced my Reuben would be ready in about three minutes. An old man was stretched across the lid of a deep freezer, snoring soundly.

We crossed the kitchen to another closed door. Beanie pushed it really hard, and finally it opened. It too had a built-in bed and built-in desk overflowing with books, files, pens, and pencils. Underneath the bed was a stack of plumbing and electrical parts. The bed was covered with a stack of foam floats with "Sargasso Bay Hotel" painted on them.

"See, I took in some homeless people after the hurricane. They pull the floats out at night and sleep on the floor of the bar after we close up. Can I count them as part of my household? I must be supporting five or six bums right now."

Oh, these tricks everyone wants to pull. I finally documented Beanie's electrical damage, as that was really all he could sort of prove. Darn shame. He'd built the building himself, and it had really held up well. I know he was secretly hoping for remodeling money, but I just couldn't stretch it that far. He was such an amicable sort of man, offering me office space in the bar and covering my tabs, so I did put down that all his appliances were apparently destroyed. He clearly needed a new freezer; what with that character sleeping on top of it, the whole lid was caved in.

Another day I went into a store and asked about 48 Queen Street. Nobody knew where it was, including the proprietor. I went next door and found out it was the store I had just been in. I mean this guy owned the place and he did not know what street he was on. When I went back to talk to him, he looked surprised, then told me he looked it up in the phone book when he filled out the forms. He always thought it was Ali's Alley. Everyone knows where Ali's Alley is, he told me.

This land had been in the family for generations, yet he couldn't remember the address. He delivered this innocent speech, as if it were quite normal not to know the name of the street where your business has been located for twenty-plus years. I mean this island is madness, the people nutty. I tell you, I never seen anything like it. I may *really* retire, after this assignment.

To compound the madness, I try to schedule an appointment for every hour. Hah! What a *joke* that is! People are always late for their appointments, as if they can't be bothered with punctuality. Many don't even *own* cars, or watches for that matter. I couldn't tell you the number of times when people have even asked me for the *date*. Last week, a guy was filling out his forms and he asked me what day it is. I told him it was the 8th. He wrote that down then asked me if I happen to know what the *month* is. I told him October, and he wrote that down. Then he asks me the *year!* Then he has the nerve to ask me if *I'm sure it's really 1995!*

I looked at my appointment book and told him to come back next Monday and he said, "You mean tomorrow?" And I had to tell him that today is *Tuesday.* He shook his head and said he was *sure* it was Sunday.

I'd tell people to meet me at the temporary FEMA office in town. Fools that we were, we thought we'd solve this address problem by having the applicants drive us to their homes so we could inspect and verify the damage. I mean, I can't believe there are people here, lived here for years, I tell you, and they never owned a car. They laughed at the suggestion and said they hitchhike or walk everywhere.

They'd show up, late of course, and look at me astonishingly when I asked them where their car was. One said, "Man, I been hitchhiking here for ten years. I never had a car." Incredibly, he lived about a half mile straight up a hill off the main road, halfway across the island. He claimed to work six days a week, always hitchhiking to and from work, though he complained about the steep hill, saying it was rough on his leg when he had to walk it. I could understand this; having met him in a tavern one night and discovering he wore a prosthesis for his right leg.

I was in the bar and this guy with the fake leg was wearing long blue jeans and work boots. The bartender was a young woman recently hired. The guy and his buddy got into a mock scuffle, and somehow his leg came loose. It appeared that one leg was sticking out at an odd angle, a foot longer than the other. This guy was screaming "Ooh, my leg!" The poor little bartender fainted and fell into the open beer cooler while the rest of the bar, who knew this guy had a fake leg, was collapsing off their bar stools in laughter. This town is weird, I tell you. Apparently that is some kind of joke they pull on newcomers to the island. Finally, they fished her out of the beer cooler, threw some rum in her face and revived her. Poor thing, what a shock she was in and everyone laughing their heads off at her.

Finally, FEMA approved us to rent cars and drive the applicants to their homes to see their damages. Since everyone is late for their appointments and I got a car now, I ask them is there somewhere more convenient to meet them besides the office. Gleefully, I am often told to meet them at a pub. So now I'm spending half my days waiting around bars for latecomers.

Beanie set me up my own table in his bar to use as my office. How very accommodating of him, but I wonder what Washington would think if they knew I'd moved my office into a bar. Of course, I've discovered several construction companies are operating out of bars too. Suspiciously, many tradesmen list their business phone number as a payphone at their favorite watering hole.

At least it is entertaining to watch how these characters operate. I notice that the employees *never* answer the bar phone. They let the customers play switchboard operator. Usually the calls are for the patrons anyhow or some tradesman, and now even me! What must my superiors think? I'm getting my calls transferred to a bar!

So one day, I was ensconced in my bar-cum-office when the phone rang and one of the especially inebriated customers answered the bar phone. I heard him say, "Bring the whole damn truck!" and hang up. I figured it must be something to do with the construction job he was on when he wasn't getting drunk.

The next day I was in the bar again, waiting for someone to show up for their appointment, late of course, and this beer distributor came in the door with a hand truck stacked with beer and an invoice which he handed to the owner of the bar who nearly had a heart attack. The bill was for a truckload of beer, priced at $22,000.

Meanwhile the same drunk (who had answered the phone, the day before) was falling down, giggling, and apologizing to the owner, saying he didn't think they'd *really* send out a truckload of beer. The beer distributor was not amused. He was a commissioned salesman, and he thought he had struck gold when he inquired as to how much beet to ship over and was told "Send the whole damn truck!"

I slid out the open doorway to drive an applicant home to inspect her damages. She had me stop at the store while she picked up groceries, then we had to pick up her laundry. She saw someone walking and insisted I stop for a moment so she could chat with them. Then as we started out of town, she implored me to pick up the hitchhikers. I wasn't sure if I should be picking up hitchhikers in a FEMA-rented vehicle, but then I said, what the hell, when in Neverland, do as the Never-landers do.

Then she directed me down this donkey trail that was cleverly disguised as a road, one that only a four-wheel vehicle could have made it up. Of course, I got stuck. I think the rental agency gave me the two-wheel drive vehicle as a joke. It took two days for a tow truck to come get my car out of that rut.

Actually, FEMA only authorized us to rent the cheapest vehicles. I had to beg and plead to get a four-wheel drive. Of course it cost a lot more, and all this had to be approved by some bureaucrat in Washington.

Anyhow, after we got stuck this lady hopped out of the car, passed me some of her laundry and groceries to carry, and we started trekking up this awful mud and rut road. We passed a lime tree and she grabbed a few fruits from it. When we got to her apartment, all the windows were blown out of it and most of the roof peeled back. Obviously she had substantial damage. As we entered through the empty frames of sliding glass doors, she astonished me by taking the laundry from me, opening up the refrigerator and setting it inside, where other clothes were neatly folded and stacked.

Her neighborhood had no electricity yet; the power company was concentrating on relighting the town before working this far up the mountain. She tossed her ice and groceries into a cooler, and then made herself a rum and rain with a squeeze of lime. (Apparently, a rum and rain is a famous post-hurricane drink consisting of rum and water. Considering that rum is cheaper than milk, juice, or soda, it's a wonder the island's kids grow up sober with food being so pricey here.)

Turns out that inside the refrigerator was the only dry spot in her apartment whenever it would rain, due to the damaged roof. So she kept her clothes and important stuff in it. She had propane gas and a stove, so she was able to cook. Numerous candles in various states of melting were scattered around, as were mosquito coils. The sink was full of dirty dishes. On the floor sat a plastic bucket. While I walked around filling out my forms on my clipboard, she picked up the bucket and walked across the tile floor to where a square was outlined.

In the middle of the square was a recessed ring. She pulled at the ring, miraculously moving a slab of concrete. With a resounding thud, she set it to the side. Then she lay on her belly across the floor and tossed her bucket into the cistern. That's when I noticed she had seven rings on her various toes and a tattoo on her ankle. With much stretching, she managed to pull up the bucket of water, with the attached thin string, splashing it and cursing at the same time.

She explained to me how she had to wash the dishes so that she could use the dirty water to flush the reeking commode. It all seemed so normal to her. I couldn't live like that, but she preferred this over staying in a public shelter, which wouldn't allow her to bring her cats.

Since her plumbing was operated by an electric pump, she had to schlep water out of the cistern. Her biggest problem, she explained to me, would be if the water ran out before the roof was repaired, seeing as the roof normally filled up the cistern with rainwater. It all looked sort of hopeless to me, but she seemed cheery enough. Two cats wandered in and out of the apartment, and she spoke to them as if they understood every word and were her precious children. Indeed, I realized now, her application *did* include two other dependents, Pinkie and BoBo. Seeing, no evidence of children, I inquired. Of *course* she listed the cats as dependents. I had to change the whole form from family to single, and she's not happy at all, now moping around.

Then there is the problem of mail addresses. Half the island seems to use the same post office box for their mail. Then, to make matters worse, most only pick up their mail every week or two. We'd send them notices for appointments and they'd come strolling in a week later, saying they just got their mail. Apparently, some people don't come into town much. One lady came all the way from Crystal Bay and said it was the first time in four years she had been to Sargasso Bay.

Phones are even worse. Most people have no phones or they are using the only answering service in town. Those people must handle messages for half the island, it seems. So I got about a thousand applications with the same phone number and the same mailing address! Our computers don't know how to handle this; the clerks are going crazy. Some folks give us a cellular number, but they never leave the phone on. We call them and get this recording that the phone is out of range or cut off.

On the few occasions when I was able to actually get through to somebody on a phone, it was never who I was looking for. I would leave a message, but most, never return calls. Now they just usually pick up their messages and meet me in the bar. They'd rather spend two dollars on a beer than twenty-five cents on a call. Go figure. Nearly every appointment that meets me has to have a drink before we can leave for their house or ruins or boat.

Tax returns. We ask people for a copy of their tax returns and they turn pale and go running out of our office. Why, the first week my caseload was cut in half, as people hastily withdrew their applications. I.D. is another problem; they fill out their application in one name and then when we ask for I.D., they pull out something like some old expired driver's license from another state and the name on it is nothing like the name on the application.

Like J.R. You hear about him? The guy that died of a heart attack last week? Everyone thought he was J.R. Mansfield and when his next of kin flew in to claim the body, he says the guy is Sherlock M. Klosky. Turns out the guy was wanted somewhere for something long ago. His family wanted him put to rest under his real name for his daughter's sake.

You tell them they forgot to put down their bank account information, and they look at me like I'm crazy. Most of these people have *never* had a bank account. They laugh at the very idea.

People tend to crowd up in their houses, and you find out you have six different cases of people applying for grants, and they all live in the same two-bedroom house.

You ask them where they work and they give you some sort of vague schedule, like Tuesdays they work at Tango's Mango, and Thursdays they work at Mumby Jumbys, and the weekends they pound nails; unless of course the surf is up, then they go to Bomba's surfing for the day.

The boat people were the oddest. Immediately, I felt sorry for them. They'd show up barefoot, wearing torn shorts and faded t-shirts with some old straw hat flopping around, looking every bit like they merely washed up ashore themselves. I was later to find out that this was acceptable daily garb for many of the boaters. One guy took me out to look at pieces of wreckage strewn on the beach. He tells me that's all he has left from his precious yacht. I asked him to show me something to identify the yacht as his. He started rummaging around the various scraps of smashed up boat debris. Then he cheerfully pulled up a shred of jagged fiberglass with half the boat name painted on it. We compare it to the picture he has from his boat-launching party the spring before. How sad. I put it down as a total loss.

Thanks to FEMA's non-discrimination against age policy, I ended up interviewing people for loans that I know they'll never be able to pay back, but through the various loopholes, they qualify for the loan just the same. So, when a salty old sailor, a former convict, lost his primary home, which happened to be a sailboat he was tired of, he miraculously qualified for a thirty year loan to buy another boat. The powerboat he secretly coveted was now a reality instead of a dream. Even though he was an ex-con, he was considered to be a good credit risk because he had a steady income. Courtesy of the government, he draws social security. The man was seventy-eight years old! This is the U.S. government, hard at work, spending your money. I'm just *Da-fema-mon*, I don't make up the rules and regulations, but it seemed funny giving this old geezer money he'd never be able to pay back from the look of the way he pickles his liver each afternoon.

Another lady had lost her home too. Also a sailboat. She too went out and purchased the sailboat of her dreams, a much nicer, sleeker one. She qualified for the thirty-year loan, which of course gave her very attractive payments.

"Can you imagine?" she said to me one day. "When I am 86, hobbling into the FEMA office on my walker with my final payment in hand, just after cashing my social security check, paying for a boat that is now thirty years *older*! Have you ever seen what thirty years can *do* to a boat!"?

Sometimes they show up and want to drive me out in this leaky dinghy that scares me half to death, to climb on their sinking vessel and look at the damage. Those were pretty scary. Our forms are designed for homes, not boats. We're trying to fill out the part about roof damage and cisterns and they're telling you their chain-plates were ripped out and I don't even *know* what a chain-plate is. One day, I'm on this woman's boat; she lives there alone. It's a nice boat, but she has some damage. It starts raining and she closes up the boat hatches and now I'm stuck, cause if we leave in the pouring rain, we will be soaked. So from her, I sort of garnered an education on life afloat. For electrical damage to the home, she volunteered her solar panel was *mash* up in the storm. Yeah, that's a new word for me. I thought it only went with mashed potatoes. But here everyone seems to tell me the hurricane *mash* their house or boat. Apparently, she powers her fan, lights, radio, and laptop computer, all off this solar contraption, which now resembles shattered glass.

When the rain finally let up, we headed back for shore. Seeing a wreck on the rocks that I knew was one of my cases, I asked her to drive by it so I could photograph it for the files. We ran aground on a piece of the wreckage, and she hopped out of the dinghy to shove us off. But she saw a part she wanted to salvage off the what-cha-ma-call-it cause it's a thingamajig she needs for her widget. Meanwhile, I was two hours late for my next appointment, not that it seems to really matter.

She pulled out this Swiss Army knife and something she called a Leatherman tool, and for twenty minutes she was struggling to get this piece off, assuring me it wouldn't matter to the owner anyhow. I wondered if we were going to get busted for looting and how would I explain *that* to my boss. Finally, she got the part off and took me back ashore.

My next case was a fifty-ish lady with a fifty-inch waistline. I felt really sorry for her after hearing her tale of woe. I almost cried right along with her. She was so sweet but had the saddest tale. When we met to look at her demolished boat, she could barely squeeze into the front seat of my jeep. I wondered how she managed to live on a boat; when she showed me a picture of her husband, I was astonished that he was even *bigger* than her. He couldn't come to the appointment cause he had been airlifted off the island to Puerto Rico. The trouble was, no one knew to which hospital. The helicopter that made the rescue failed to note his name or which hospital they sent him to. She was anxiously awaiting news by cellular phone at the floral shop. Seems the owner there had her father, who lived in Puerto Rico, looking for the guy. San Juan has a load of community hospitals, and this guy was tracking them all down, but no word yet.

Her husband had ended up injured in the hurricane because he stayed on the boat. Their entire life savings were tied up in this boat. They were pushing sixty and everything they owned in the whole world now lay in a destroyed heap on a rocky remote beach. So remote that I had to stand on the cliff overlooking it, with a pair of binoculars to see her shattered boat below. It was either that or repel down by rope, which at my age, I had no intention of doing, thank-you.

I asked her how she escaped injury and she told me before the hurricane, they had this massive argument. He wanted to stay on board, and she wanted to stay ashore with friends. In the end, they stayed separately. Throughout the storm, she was frantic, wondering if her husband or boat would survive. After the storm, she went out to the beach at Great Cruz Bay to see if she could find her boat and husband. Both were gone and she began asking questions of everyone around.

Seems that during the height of the storm, the boat broke free of her anchors and was blowing out of the harbor. Her husband apparently donned a pair of flippers to swim for shore. He miraculously made it to shore, but all his clothes were torn off of him, along with a hunk of his rear end. He ended up knocking on the door to a beachside hotel. The guests answered the door and were shocked to see a naked man with two flippers, one in front and one in back, standing there dripping wet and bleeding. When the storm was over, he was wrapped in a sheet and air lifted to Puerto Rico. Between sobs, she explained she had lost her home, her life's savings, her business, and now her husband was missing. I almost cried right along with her. Needless to say, they are getting maximum help, which they surely deserve.

Another day I went out with a couple to see their house—or ruins, I should politely say. It was absolutely incredible. We were standing at the top of this hill, where their cistern still stood, however, the house was scattered down to the east in a heap of rubble. I took his word for it that it used to be his two-bedroom house. I asked him how on earth his family survived. He pointed to a lone couch sitting down off to the west propped up against a leafless tree.

"You see, during the storm, we made some bagels and cream cheese. The three of us were sitting on our brand new couch; I mean it was just delivered two days before the storm. All of a sudden, there is this terrible noise as the house disintegrated; first the roof, then the walls gave away. I threw myself over my wife and daughter for protection; the wind and rain was howling around us. We got blown down that hill, scream-ing all the way, and our house blew off the other way. A miracle, don't you think?"

Yes, a miracle, I think. Thank God for mira-cles. Another couple was not so lucky. They had to be dug out of their house and though they were both still alive, the sight of them was not pretty at all. They were airlifted to a Puerto Rico hospital too.

Then there was the truck woman. A strange lot she was. She was living in this truck with all her belongings stashed under a tarp in back. She slept in the front seat of the cab at night and cooked under a banyan tree by day with a portable camp stove. She drove her truck out to the campground for a shower when she needed one. I asked her how she ended up living in the truck. Seems that before the first hurricane slammed the island, she had decided to move to another island. She had hired a local guy who owned a big flatbed truck to come pack her up and move her, by way of barging the truckload over to the other island. They got her all packed up, but it was too late to make the last ferry over to the other island. The next day, the hurricane threats were issued and the barges were not run-ning, as they were sailing for a hurricane hole to hide in. So, she stayed in a hotel during the storm, and her belongings stayed in the truck. Meanwhile, after the hurricane, the truck owner wanted to dump her belongings because he had lots of people wanting to rent his truck to clean up their mess or to rebuild their mess or to move their mess.

She was adamant that her stuff stay on the truck and be delivered over to the next island. The truck owner was none too happy about this, but within two more days the barges were running again. So he took the truck on the barge. When they get to her new house, a huge tree that had fallen from the storm blocked the road to it. The truck owner was not going to lug all her belongings by hand over the tree. He went out in search of a chain saw. By now, this woman and her belongings have tied up his truck for over a week. He was anxious to get her stuff unloaded and start making the high dollars of having his truck booked day and night by others who desperately wanted to make hurricane repairs.

When he finished clearing the tree off the road with a rented chain saw, he was much too tired to unload the truck or to go home. The lady slept on the floor in her new house, and he slept in the truck's cab. The next morning, they unloaded all her belongings into the house. He was relieved. She still had business back on St John, so she rode with him back to the ferry dock to take the barge over on the truck. But, alas, the second hurricane was then coming, and the barges had once again left to go in hiding. They were now stuck on a different island for the second hurricane. They drove back to her new house with a load of groceries, and he stayed in her house with her for the storm. He was fuming; she's now had his truck tied up for eleven days. Wait until she gets *his* moving bill, he thought.

The storm got so rough that part of the house gave away, and they found themselves huddled in the bathtub together, the bathroom being the strongest room of the house. After that hurricane passed, her house was severely damaged. She no longer wanted to live there. So the trucker agreed to load up the remainder of her belongings and barge the stuff back over to St John. On the way over to the ferry dock, they got stuck in a traffic jam that lasted until well past the barge's departure time. They spent the night in the truck together, neither too happy about the arrangement. They ran out of cigarettes and nearly killed each other, but somehow survived the night.

The next morning, they were able to finally make it to the barge and go over to the next island. Much to their horror, the damage is substantial and she hasn't a clue where to deposit her belongings. She wanted to leave them on the truck, and he wanted them off so that he could go earn some more money. He quoted her a ridiculously high bill, which resulted in a raucous argument. He threatened to take her stuff to the dump. In the end she just bought the truck off of him. Now she's living in it on St John, but her damaged house is on St. Thomas. She cussed me out in three different languages when I told her she has to file with the other FEMA office on the other island because that is where her last home was.

Insurance. Why is it so few seem to have insurance? Most folks laugh in our face when we ask about insurance. I find out it is ridiculously high, as some pointed out to me, it is either insurance for the home or groceries for the table. On the loans over ten thousand dollars, FEMA requires they get insurance on their property. Suddenly they don't want the twenty thousand dollar loan, and settle for the ten because they don't want to be stuck with ridiculously high insurance payments.

I feel for them. The government has various methods of determining the loans and such, sometimes with common sense clearly thrown out the window. One guy, he had thirty thousand in estimates to rebuild his house, so we approved a loan for twenty thousand based on his income, or reportable income I should say; he was a bartender that claimed he made no tips at all, not a one the whole year. He claimed this because none were shown on his tax return. We knew from the looks of his former lifestyle that he must have made a good deal in tips, but he didn't report it and we couldn't count it.

We told him to go get insurance and he came back the next day, saying that is going to cost him eight thousand and only leave him twelve thousand against thirty thousand in damages. So he settled for the ten thousand dollar loan. Now this loan was supposed to go for the home repairs only. The next week I saw him driving a fancy pick-up truck with a tarp in back and some nails. I admonished him that his loan was *not* for a new pickup truck. He said he bought the truck to haul the tarp and nails home, since he can't afford to rebuild the roof anyhow.

I tell you, after this stint, I am *retiring* to a place with *street* addresses and *private phones* and people who own cars and shoes and actually *know* where they live and perhaps even what day it is. This place is making me nutty!

Bartender! Another rum and rain, please!

My First Murder

The blazing sun was just starting to set across the Caribbean Sea. I paused on the deck of my sailboat to watch it for a few moments. As the zenith slowly sank on the horizon, I squinted my eyes searching for the elusive green flash. Poof! It looked like a bright flashbulb glimmering for a millisecond on the horizon, and then the sun was gone.

I returned to my chores in the boatyard, where my boat was high and dry. For the first time in years, I was leaving my small live-aboard sailboat to fend for herself in the yard for a few months.

Setting off a can of Woebegone Bug Bomb in the cabin, I scrambled to close the companionway boards, locking them securely. Everything from the deck was already stored below or securely tied. I climbed down the ladder, saying a silent good-bye to my home. I felt confident she could weather a hurricane on shore. Last year we had survived three hurricanes in the water. Her paint job, anchor rodes (and my nerves) were all a little worse for wear.

Summer flew by as I spent my time working atop a mountain over two thousand miles away. There I became known as *that-woman-who-lives-on-a-sailboat-in-the-Caribbean.* As fall crept closer, I looked forward to returning to my floating home.

The evening I arrived back on the island, I got my rusty old jeep running after jump-starting the battery. Gleefully driving to the boatyard, I was curious to see how my vessel had fared. So far, no hurricanes had struck the island this year; just a few scares. Under the light of the moon, I combed the yard from one end to the other looking in vain for my boat. In the space where I had last seen her sat a mono-hull much larger than mine. I circled the yard again, finding no sign of her.

Glumly, I walked to the Slip Away, a well-known, local watering hole for wayward sailors. It sits propped on stilts by the ocean's edge. The place is open-air, having only a wooden half-wall around the edges to corral in the drunks. Even so, occasionally an inebriated soul managed to fall out of the bar, landing on the soft sand below. Recently, thick ropes had been strung from pillar to post to rein in the partying patrons, but still the odd one fell out.

A sign on the wall read "Don't toss your cigarettes on the floor, it burns the hands and knees of departing patrons."

I walked up the breezy stairway. Josiah, the bartender gave me a warm welcome. Half a dozen people at the bar turned to look, a few of them smiled and waved. Three people were sitting on the wall, sipping from their bottles and leaning into the safety-rope. They briefly held their beers aloft in a mock toast to my entrance, a bit of a welcome back gesture.

Ordering a glass of wine, I pulled a stool up to the bar, commanding an excellent view of the Caribbean Sea. Warm zephyrs wafted through the club, carrying off hints of perfume, sweat, and cigarettes coupled with garlicky cooking odors from the kitchen. A large catamaran was negotiating the narrow channel into the marina with tourists dancing on the deck to a loud rumba. Two hours earlier, they had soberly left on a sunset cruise. Several complimentary rounds of Pirate's Rum Punch made the sunset look extraordinarily spectacular, their partners hilariously entertaining, and the dance music oh so enticing. All just like the brochure promised.

Josiah set down a glass of Concha Y Toro vino. I took a small sip. He stood there, smiling broadly, his bright teeth contrasting with his dark skin.

"How's t'ings? Your boat okay?"

"Can't find it. "

"Can't find it! Oh boy!" He roared with laughter.

"Did you look in de' graveyard?"

"Of course not. Tell me. How could the boat-yard *lose* a thirty-foot sailboat?"

"Oh, she in da' graveyard!" He grinned at me, chuckling merrily, as if he'd just heard a hilarious joke.

"The graveyard! But. . . but. . . but, I *paid my* bill!"

This was met with a rowdy round of laughter from the other drinkers. I still didn't get the joke, but it was definitely on me. I was thinking of the graveyard. It is an untended piece of land across the road from the boatyard proper. Vessels that are derelicts or presumed abandoned, perhaps because storage payments had not been forthcoming from the last-known owner, were moved there. Some were vandalized by scavengers or sold off at a pitiful auction to pay the past due storage. Over the years, unlucky crafts had met their eventual death there, hence the lovely nickname bestowed upon it, the Grave Yard.

"Oh, is not da' graveyard anymore, is now all fenced in and locked up. D'ey say it's the best place to be, mon. " Josiah giggled, as if I should *know* this myself.

"I can't believe they put me in the Grave Yard! The only good thing about that part of the yard is the breeze from the ocean just feet away. A high surf during a hurricane would have floated the boat right offshore!"

"No, mon. D'ey put up d'e fence. Your boat not going anywhere. She safe d'ere. I think d'ey even put in current and water too."

"Wow. The graveyard has electricity now?"

"Yeah, mon, d'ey got current."

I nursed my drink, pondering why my boat had been moved there. Two glasses of wine later, I walked to the graveyard. True to Josiah's word, there was a new fence bordering an old double gate that hung at odd angles. It was locked up tight with chain and padlock. Only an anorexic super-model could have squeezed into the gap. About three dozen boats were tightly packed in the graveyard.

I could barely see a tiny glitter of my forty-two foot mast. The sloop was parked right next to the beach, her stern facing it and the rest of her surrounded by closely parked boats. I walked around the fence, looking longingly through the wire at peek-a-boo glimpses of my home. It was getting late. I drove to the other end of the island, where I camped out on a friend's couch in his tiny apartment.

The next morning I arrived at the boatyard so early that no one else had arrived to work. I went for breakfast, returning later. The new manger had the key to the graveyard, but he was not around. Several stops throughout the day did not wield any success. It was early fall, hurricane season was not quite over, and it would be another month or so before work in the boat yard picked up steadily.

The next day, I met the new yard manager. He tossed around his desk until he found the magic key. I skipped my way across the rut-filled road to the gate. The lock was in bad need of oiling. After nearly spraining my wrist, I finally managed to open the lock, practically breaking the key off in the midst of opening the rusty hunk of metal.

I ran over to my sailboat, almost ready to kiss her, I was so happy to see her alive and well! Not only was she backed up as close to the fence as they could have parked her, but her solar panel was completely shaded by a palm frond that carefully covered every square inch.

I sighed. I groaned. I sweated in the mid-morning sun, pondering the probability of dead batteries. Usually the solar panel kept my batteries topped up to run the fans, lights, pressure water, stereo and vacuum cleaner. Anxious to climb aboard, I hiked around the tall grassy yard, searching for a ladder to use. Finding one, it was of course handmade. Whoever made it didn't care much for right angles or levels, so it was rather rickety, but the best I could find. This particular yard refused to buy pre-engineered manufactured ladders, preferring to give the task of building them to their least competent carpenter.

I dragged it back through the scrub brush, rearranging unused boat props and dodging other obstacles along the way. Leaning it against the stern of the boat, I took in a long deep breath. I hate ladders. I retied my sarong into a shorter skirt then clamored up the shaky treads, saying a long plaintive prayer as I ascended.

Nervously I negotiated my way aboard, perspiration pouring profusely down my face and neck, soaking through my top. It was 97 degrees in the shade, over 100 in the sun, and the humidity seemed about equal. Ropes ran across the cockpit every which way, firmly tying down the boom and the bimini frame.

Contorting my sweaty body, I somehow managed to weave through the myriad of lines to the starboard side. Opening the shallow locker, I dug through bits of lines, old muddy anchor gloves, sun lotion bottles, chafe gear, flares, a water cap key on a floating key chain, a pair of vice grips, and miscellaneous boat gear until I located my set of keys, at the very bottom of the locker, of course.

I opened the boat, while sweat ran rivers down my burning face. I paused momentarily to catch my breath while mopping my brow, letting the vessel air herself out.

Removing the vertical hatch boards, I looked down into the boat and was absolutely mortified!

Little dark things littered the entire place. They looked like dead bugs. Gee, I thought, that Woebegone spray sure worked effectively. Funny, I had no bugs when I left. They must have snuck aboard, found the intoxicating spray, then promptly dropped dead. Gingerly stepping down the steps gave me a complete view of my galley. It was in shambles. I was shocked, totally unnerved before I realized that *rats* had been literally shredding my worldly goods. All my precious spice bottles, the hand-blown, green glass ones with thick cork tops, were minutely minced, their contents spread all over the cabin quite generously. Plastic bottles had their lids chewed away, the fragments liberally scattered about the countertops and sole.

The little black things I mistook for dead bugs, were in fact, nasty rat turds from some mighty prolific rats. It looked like they had a swell party during my absence. They must have stowed away onboard before I left a few months earlier. I had unwittingly locked them inside. From what I could tell, there was no evidence of their entrance. Meaning that they had no way to escape, either. Horrors!

As I surveyed the damages, I imagined their tale of two tails:

Super-Rat ate the vitamins.
Saucy-Rat dined on the spices.
Dopey-Rat gobbled the pain pills.

Sushi-Rat munched the Nori and wasabi.
Bulk-Rat crunched the Grape Nuts.

A fury leg stepped on the button for the radio, letting that play until it drained the batteries completely. (Had the palm frond not lovingly shielded my solar panel, the rats could have had four months of pure musical bliss.)

I was amazed at the damage these varmints had wreaked on my precious home. It was hard to tell if it was two or ten rats invading the place.

I stood there and cried. There was nowhere to sit down that was not already covered in rat droppings. Closing up the companionway, I drove to town in a mild state of shock. I was intent on buying six rattraps, ten glue-traps, and a case of poison bait. War was declared; just let me load up on ammunition!

My preference was for the glue-traps, so I could capture the rotters alive and torture them. (Just kidding!) Shopping is frustrating at times in the islands, mon, t'ings come and t'ings go. I went into the grocery store. Could not find a trap or poison. I approached the cashier.

"Excuse me, do you have rat traps or poison?"

"Finish. You sure you got rats? We got bug spray. Try d'at. "

I thanked her and left, *finish* is the islanders' term for *out-of-stock-heaven-knows-when-we-will-ever-get-more and if we ever do, it probably won't be this year.*

At the next grocery store, another customer overheard me asking the clerk about rattraps and poison. He interjected himself into the conversation as the clerk wandered off. He told me *exactly* what to do.

"What you do is, you disconnect the exhaust hose from the engine of your boat. Then you fire it up, and close up the cabin tightly. The interior will fill up with carbon monoxide and suffocate the bastards. *That's* how you kill a rat!" His eyes glimmered, his face dead serious. He wore fatigue pants, and a knife was sheathed in a leather holder on his belt. A chain was attached to his wallet, then his belt loop. A canteen was strung from his shoulder, as was a small backpack. His long sleeve shirt had pockets down the front and on the sleeves. Each appeared to have something stuffed in them. Another veteran from a different war, lurking in the islands. I politely thanked him, supposing the scheme had merit if you didn't mind all that smoke ruining the interior.

I went to Whitney's Department Store. A clerk approached me on aisle three.

"Can I help you?"

"Do you have rat poison or traps?"

"Oh, do not use poison! You have rats in your house?"

"No, on my boat."

"If you use poison, that rat will pick the most *inopportune* place to die on the inside of the hull, one that is completely inaccessible, except by chain saw. Then it will reek and stink for months on end, making it totally uninhabitable. Don't use poison. Use traps, they're better. Then you just toss them into a bucket of water, 'til they drown. You'll know, when the bubbles stop coming up, they be *real* dead, mon."

"Great! Where are your rat-traps?"

"Finish. Try Filbert's Dry Goods, you know just past the roundabout next to Pappa Doodles Fish Fry?"

At Filbert's I got a lesson in economics. I asked the clerk for rattraps or poison. In a typically nonsensical way, she offered the perfect explanation.

"We quit carrying d'ose because we couldn't keep d'em on d'e shelf. We get a load in, and d'en d'ey finish."

"People don't like to see an empty store, so we only order stuff we can keep on the shelves. Never can keep d'ose on d'e shelves."

Wow, this was certainly turning out to be an entertaining and educational but rather ineffective shopping trip.

At the next store I searched all the shelves, then woke up the clerk, who was napping with his head down on the counter by the register.

"Do you have rat-traps or glue-traps or rat poison?"

"Finish" was his one word reply before he laid his head back down.

"When will you be getting more in?"

He picked his head up with great effort.

"When de boat come in, mon."

"When will that be?"

He looked at me like I was some kind of slow-witted moron.

"Next month, maybe. Or did it already come d'is month. I forget. When it come, it come."

He slowly closed his eyes, laying his head back down.

My next stop was a dusty old hardware store in a residential neighborhood. It was dimly lit, with an eclectic mixture of merchandise randomly scattered on dingy shelves. The eighty-something-year-old clerk stood up from behind the counter where she was perusing the weekly paper. Her thick eyeglasses enlarged her almond-shaped eyes, making them appear to bulge out of their sockets. She solemnly nodded at my request.

After shuffling up and down a few darkened aisles, she stopped and pointed to a lone box at the back of a lower shelf. I squatted down, and reached as far as I could and managed to grab the filthy little box. Possibly the *only* rat poison for sale on the entire island. At the cash register, she picked up a cloth and carefully dusted the box like I'd just purchased a museum show-piece.

Back at the yard, I was surprised to see that no one had nicked my ladder. I'd completely forgotten to tie it off to the stern. Quickly, I went down below, leaving my tasty treats out for the rats. I tied the ladder to the stern pulpit, then started to leave, but changed my mind.

I forced myself to throw out several bags of rat-damaged stuff. They had managed to chew up every plastic bottle in the boat including shampoo, conditioner, aloe lotion, and even toothpaste. Colored, shell-shaped bars of soap were grotesquely gnawed around the edges. I bagged it all up for the dump, then left for the day, careful to leave a choice of openings for the poisoned rats to escape by.

The next day, I checked on the rat feast. Green poison pellets were liberally scattered around each feeding box. They had greedily devoured the poison in haste, not bothering with neatness. For good measure, they had shredded the cardboard box the poison came in. They must have been ravenous! From the amount of poison ingested, I expected that dead rats would be flopped-out everywhere. Were they lazing around somewhere, in dark recesses, dying to stink up my boat? Arming myself with a hefty meat clever, I tentatively began cleaning. It was heart breaking to bag up all this garbage, stuff that only vaguely resembled my once treasured belongings.

Maid-rat had used a whole roll of paper towels to line various parts of the cabinets, coupled with bits of cork, spices, and debris. Keeping a watchful eye, I nervously opened up various lockers with one hand, while brandishing the meat cleaver in the other, as if silly old me would actually do battle with a rat! The heft of the cleaver made me feel a bit foolish, as I sorted items with the other hand, throwing things to either the garbage pile or "the keepers." Thanks to the extensive damage to my personal belongings, I was gaining all sorts of empty storage area as the pile of garbage turned into a small mountain.

After filling up two more garbage bags, I called it a day. It was incredibly hot, no breeze in sight, and the ocean like a glassy lake. I went swimming for a long time, trying to wash away my revulsion of cleaning up the damages and rat droppings.

In the morning I entered the graveyard, nodding at several workers who were busy with loud grinders. Blue paint chips were flying around them, as they worked on the shady side of a boat. I climbed aboard my boat. The workers never heard my screaming over the din of their power tools.

There was a rat! Sitting in the middle of the cabin sole! I banged the bulkhead loudly to let him know I was there. He looked at me, limply crawled about three inches, with one ear wiggling.

The devil was weak from the gluttony of his ways! Grabbing a bucket, I gingerly stepped across the sole, placing it over the sick scoundrel. He wiggled around, his grossly long tail flicked out from under the edge of the overturned bucket, resembling a little snake. I screamed unprintable obscenities at him, as his tail continued to swish around. The rechargeable drill was sitting out on the table. It seemed the only heavy thing handy, so I placed it atop the bucket, then fled the boat.

Now, I wanted some macho male to come help me out. Like get that thing *off* my boat. I walked over to the grinders, smiling. When I told them my story-with-request, they thought it highly amusing. Claiming that they had to finish that job first, they'd come by on their lunch break.

Sure.

I crossed the yard, running into Denzil. I asked him for help. He declared I should just wait until the rat died naturally, and then toss him out.

Uh, huh.

Well, you can hardly blame people for being far too busy with their own tasks to assist in evicting a rat. Perhaps I'd go to lunch, mull this problem over. Walking past the dumpster, I noticed a cardboard case sitting on top. I retrieved it and did a three-sixty, heading back to my boat.

Stealthily I climbed back aboard, armed with my cardboard. I began to slide it under the bucket, forgetting that my cabin sole is slightly curved.

YIKES!

The rat escaped!

Screaming profanities, I chased the feeble scalawag across the floor, recapturing him with my trusty bucket. Then I slid the cardboard under him, and he was trapped. My heart beat wildly threatening to exit my rib cage with its incessant throbbing.

The phone rang. I kid you not. I use a cellular for my business. Tucked in my backpack, it was ringing again. Calmly, I stepped over the bucket, answering with as cheery a "Good afternoon" as I could muster. It was a client, inquiring about my catering services. We chatted amicably as my bucket began dancing around the cabin sole as the rat tried to escape his confines. Without screaming into my caller's ear, I managed to calmly terminate the phone call after a few pleasantries about talking in the near future.

Grabbing the toolbox, I put it across the bucket to weigh it down. His awful tail swung about wildly. I cursed at him in every language I know. I tried to pick up the bucket and cardboard, discovering I needed four hands. Thinking fast, I lunged for my roll of duct tape (a must-have for anyone living in the islands). I securely taped the overturned bucket to the cardboard base, with the dreaded rat inside.

Picking up the improvised trap, I made it as far as the cockpit. Deciding I had had enough, I just flung the whole mess overboard where it landed with a thud on the grass below. Mind you, my deck was about ten feet in the air. I hoped he had died during the harsh landing.

But the old Scottish in me wanted my bucket back! Otherwise, some scavenger would come along and surely take it for him or herself (of course, he/she might be shocked to find it housed a dying rat). Boldly I climbed down the ladder and strolled over to the contraption where I firmly put my foot atop the overturned bucket and ripped off all the tape. Then I gave the bucket a good kick. The sluggish rat managed to slowly crawl, amazingly, back into the bucket, which landed on its side.

I was now in a murderous rage, out of control. Spying a rock nearby, I seized it while flinging the rat out of my precious bucket. I threw the rock at him for good measure, but he continued to wiggle. Grabbing the rock again, I heaved it at the repulsive creature, which dared to wreck my little home. Still, he showed signs of life. Losing my head all together, I repeatedly smashed him with the rock, and then set it atop him, jumping up and down on the rock till he was mashed thoroughly. As if on cue, the loud grinders shut down, the operators sauntered off. They hadn't noticed a thing.

The rat lay still. I was shaking worse than a palm frond in a hurricane. Managing to stumble across the yard, I ran into the new manager at the gate's edge. He looked at me curiously, inquiring about my current health. Telling him my tale of woe, he found it exceedingly hilarious. At the moment, I saw no humor at all in what I had done. Continuing onward with my vibrating gait, I slumped into a chair at the Slip Away. Amidst the busy lunchtime crowd, I drank a Jack Daniels and Coke. Two to be exact, to calm my addled nerves. Once my hands were steady again, I ordered a hamburger to soak up the alcohol sloshing around my dubious tummy.

Eventually, I stumbled back to my sailboat, bravely going aboard as if I owned the place (I do, well, I sort of share ownership with various credit cards; boats ain't cheap, and I ain't rich either). Somehow, my sarong caught on something; the material gave way as I heard a small r-r-i-i-p-p. Darn. I looked down at the tear, wondering if I had a spare sarong in the jeep. Meanwhile, I swept up more rat turds, bagging up garbage and laundry along the way. The rats had not bothered my linens or clothes, but I just felt bound to wash *everything* these varmints had touched.

Toward the end of the day, I gently threw the garbage and laundry down into the yard, so I wouldn't have to negotiate the ladder with them. I opened up the port cockpit locker, digging deeply until I found the 100-foot extension cord. I planned to plug in the borrowed battery charger to run overnight since I'd found the newly installed *current.* Looking longingly at the ocean, I thought a swim in short order would feel just right. I heard a noise. Suddenly there was a tall dark man, clinging to my ladder with one hand, holding a sharpened machete in the other.

"Good afternoon!" he bade me. Funny, I'm thinking that's awfully polite for a pirate. I *knew* this graveyard was bad luck! Oh, what the hell. I answered him.

"Good afternoon."

"Da' manager said sumthin' about cutting a palm frond d'at be in your way. D'is be da' one?" He pointed with his machete at the frond covering my solar panel.

"Why, thank you, yes that's the one."

He began hacking away at it. I turned back to the open locker, stuffed the water hose, life jackets, and fenders back inside then closed it. As I straightened up, I nearly jumped three feet. Sitting on the cockpit coaming, pretty as you please, was a rat! We eyed each other. It was breathing heavy, trying to plod down the deck.

"Ugh!" I hollered.

"A rat!" I pointed to the offending creature.

The man paused from his gardening, his eyes grew wide, and he seemed to lose his grip on the ladder momentarily.

"Kill it!" I implored. After all, I thought, I killed the *last* one.

He climbed into the cockpit, inquiring if I had an old rag. I vainly looked around the cockpit. I saw the tear in my sarong, so I finished ripping a hunk out of it, exposing my pale thigh. He looked startled as I passed it to him.

"Use this."

"You want d'is back?"

"No! Just *kill it!*" I imagined he was planning on covering the despicable rodent up before he pierced its evil little heart with the machete.

My eyes widened as he reached over with the colorful cloth, *picking the rat up!* He flung it expertly in a high arc. The rodent sailed past the palm tree, over the chain-linked fence and across the small sandy beach, and landed twenty yards offshore, splashing loudly in the crystal clear waters.

We watched intently as the rat made an unceremonious dive and sank. The cloth fluttered after him like a parachute after an ill-fated landing. We were engrossed with the scene, totally absorbed, keeping our eyes trained on the spot where he went in. The wind was very calm, the sea flat. The ripples continued to fan out in perfect circles. The rag slowly sank out of sight. We saw neither hide nor hair of the rat. After a few silent minutes, we turned to look at each other. Before I could utter a word, he summed it all up for both of us.

"Finish."

Not All Blow Jobs Are Hurricanes

It was after 1:00 a.m., and I was nervous to be out on the street alone. My ex-boyfriend had recently had a double hernia operation. I had invited him to recuperate on my boat, but in the condition he was in after surgery, there was no way he could climb in and out of the dinghy, much less up the top side of the boat. So he booked a room at the Tamarind Court. They had generously given him a 20% discount.

We had sat in the bar drinking, and he was mixing his alcohol with his pain pills to see what kind of high he could get, as well as trying to relieve the intense pain of a double hernia operation. He took the key to his room from the bartender, and I helped him up the stairs to the room. It was furnished with the skinniest single bed I had ever seen. One lone chair and a rickety nightstand with a lamp completed the ensemble. A lone picture with the frame coming apart at the corners was hung crookedly on the wall.

Obviously, I would not be spending the night with him as we had both hoped, even though we knew any sort of intimacy would be out of the question. The bathroom was located down the hallway. Since I lived aboard a boat, he offered me a free shower. I tiptoed down the hallway and showered, then returned to his room.

He left for a shower and came back wrapped in a towel. He sat on the cot and I in the chair as we smoked the last of a joint someone had donated his way. He slipped the towel off and I was quietly horrified to see his balls swelled up to four times their normal size. He had twin incisions from the double hernia operation. Groaning, he unscrewed the pill bottle and swallowed another pain pill and stretched out. We talked a few more minutes. Realizing the tiny chair would be far too uncomfortable for me to sleep in, I decided to depart.

Outside the wind rustled the tamarind trees, and a fountain trickled down a lone statue. A calico cat stretched languidly and then chased a lizard across the courtyard. I strolled across the courtyard and out the gate. Glancing at my watch I was shocked to see that it was after 1:00 a.m. Taking a deep breath, I remembered my previous self-defense training. One, keep your wits about you; two, carry your key ring splayed between your fingers; three, walk straight and tall, hold your head high, and try not to appear drunk.

I remember the instructor telling us how punching out an eyeball was equivalent to punching your fingers into a bowl of Jell-O. I wondered how he knew. He had shown us how to direct a blow to just below the nose, and if it was hard enough we might send the nose bone back into the brain and not only disable the attacker but kill him too. He taught us the classic knee jerk, delivered to the groan of the facing attacker. He demonstrated how to kick the shins or stomp hard on the toes if the attacker was behind. Always it was "attack, stun, and run." "Attack stun, and run." No need to stick around picking a bigger fight. Feets get moving.

All this was rambling around my rum-clouded brain as I stepped out of the Tamarind Gate and into the street. In this part of town the sidewalks were far and few between, forcing one to alternately walk in the street and off again and sometimes down a path of dirt. Certain obstacles such as a tree or phone pole would force me back in the lane of traffic. Other rum-clouded souls were shakily finding their way home. Drinking alcohol is a popular sport and way of life on St. John for many. The roads are mostly horrible, twisty lanes with a potpourri of potholes and obstacles, such as a car parked in the street, forcing people to drive at a fairly slow speed. Hence, the police, who take a very leisurely attitude towards work to start with, pretty much ignore this ritual of drinking and driving.

But fortunately, the town's bars, two dozen, more or less, are all located within about four blocks of each other. So it is entirely possible to stumble and roam around the town at night, visiting several places with ease. Carrying a drink in hand is entirely acceptable as you shuffle along to the next stop to see who is there, what is going on, or to search in vain for a cheaper drink, or maybe to look for someone, with a message in mind.

But this was mid-week and off-season and all were already drunk by midnight, so all the bars had closed up by the time I trekked down the hill and into the tiny town. My dinghy was tied up at the docks on the other side of town. A few minutes into the walk, I saw a well-dressed woman up ahead of me, trudging a bit slowly. So I sped up my own pace, but not so fast as to alarm her, so I could perhaps have company on this late-night walk. I had never been out in town after everything was closed. I assumed nothing went on, but was I ever wrong. A very different life was happening in the middle of the night. Insomniacs apparently drive through the town, some with sex for hire on their mind.

"Good evening!" I called as I neared her. She had on a cute mini-dress that seemed to be custom-made to her curves. She was a dark-skinned woman with the most incredible body, very well proportioned, like a top model or movie star. She turned toward me and I saw that her face was surprisingly plain, not striking at all, but adorned with expertly applied lipstick in a hue coordinated to her coloring. Her eyes were round and equally dark.

"Good evening," she replied, as she looked me up and down and from head to toe, appraising me completely, a most unusual act from woman to woman, I thought; but then I had certainly noticed her drop-dead body as I approached, wishing that I looked like that, and realizing it was genetically impossible. So I thought it comical, she should take-in my dress, radically different from hers on a decidedly different type of body, light-skinned, with a year round tan. I had long dark hair bound in a single French braid and wore a thick, gold choker necklace around my neck. My purple and black sarong with fringe was tied around my shoulders, complimented by my utilitarian "fake-in-stocks" as I often called them; or rather, shall I say, leather, rubber-soled sandals ergonomically designed for walking and traversing by accepting the foot as a natural thing and molding the shoe to the foot rather than vice versa.

"Where are you going?" she asked as we continued to walk in stride, on and off the roadside and sometimes sidewalk.

"To the ferry dock; my dinghy is tired up near there. I live on a boat in the harbor. I've never been out this late before. I see town is closed."

"Yeah," she replied, "Town is closed, but I walk with you. Is best you not be out here alone after town is closed. Crazy people out this time of night."

I laughed nervously and thought about inquiring where she was going. Before I could say another thing, a car slowed up behind us and an old West Indian man hung out the window. "Babe! How about a ride? Get in!" he called, as he leered at the woman next to me, then glanced at me and back at her again, smiling a hopeful, toothless grin at us.

"I'm busy, not now. Good night, later," she answered him, not at all surprised at the verbal transaction. Her stride never really slowed, and I paced myself with her as we began to cross a side street and approach a paved sidewalk that ran down the length of the fenced-in ball-field. Now we wouldn't have to do battle with the oncoming traffic for road space. I was a bit surprised at the amount of traffic, jeeps, trucks, cars, and the lone taxi without passengers. Where were all these people going if town had closed over an hour and a half ago? By all rights, I figured everyone to be home in bed, or at least in *somebody's* bed by this hour. An old blue, green, and brown rusty truck approached us from the other direction. It tooted and slowed down and looked over expectantly at me and my walking companion.

"No, I'm busy, I see you later," she said to him, as we continued down the sidewalk. I was looking at him sideways, thinking hmmm...

We approached a fork in the road where there was an overhanging tamarind tree of immense breadth. Even though a streetlight was nearby, a rarity, the tree completely blocked out all the light to the street. The road curved and forked, and we were plunged into total darkness as we crossed over and took the right fork, strolling under the massive tree branches. Another car came from behind us, slowed down, and the anonymous driver said, "You need a ride? Hop in, darling."

She waved him off, half turning toward the car, "No thanks, see you later." I marveled at the number of men that wanted to give her a ride home. She was dressed very nicely, so I asked her where she worked, thinking she must be a hostess or something at a little club around here, one I had yet to set foot in.

"Here," she said. "Those were my customers."

"Oh!" was all I could manage to say as I wondered about just what this might mean. My brain was, as I mentioned earlier, plied with rum and fortified with a joint, and it was the latest I had been out at night in a long time. We approached the main intersection of town. This consisted of two one-way, one-lane streets, where traffic alternately stopped from the two directions to drive in two different directions, each street being one way and all. On one corner stood the only bank on the island and across from it the communications center, aptly named Connections.

By day, one could stand on any of the four corners, and probably manage to speak with half the people in town eventually, as everyone had to pass through this four-corner intersection to enter or depart from the smallish town. Usually pedestrians are given the right-of-way, but sometimes, impatient tourists in rental jeeps, their eyes wide as they struggled to remember drive on the left, not right, would plow through the intersection and nearly kill a pedestrian.

The other reason for stopping at the four corners was to speak to someone on the corner, to look around and see who is where, so why not let the pedestrian have right of way and pause for a stop and look-see. The corner we approached would have traffic coming from our right and left.

Sure enough, a jeep and an old Oldsmobile so low to the ground you wondered how he negotiated the pot-holed roads both stopped. Both vied for the attention of my walking companion, and it struck me as comical that I was out at nearly 2:00 a.m. now strolling with a hooker, a lady of the night. Working for money to pay for her fancy clothes and possibly lavish lifestyle.

Who knows why a woman turns to prostitution for a living. It never bothered me, the fact that there are prostitutes, both male and female. It is the oldest profession besides motherhood— I think it was Erma Bombeck who said motherhood was older. But it had never occurred to me there were prostitutes in Cruz Bay, working it by night after the town was closed.

I once had a good friend for many years who was a call girl in my former hometown. I thought of her and her skewed perspective of life, men and sex.

We crossed the corner after she bade the soliciting customers a good night and headed toward the ferry dock, which was brightly lit up ahead. So I asked her name and she mumbled something I could not understand so I asked again.

"Babe is what they call me," she said, jerking her upturned thumb over her shoulder, towards the last calling customer, and then added, "Marbella is my true name."

So I told her my name as we approached the ferry dock. "Nice to meet you, Marbella," I said, and I stuck out my hand, and we shook hands.

"Nice to meet you too," she said. I walked down the side ramp and out to the dinghy dock.

"Good night," she called.

"Good night" I replied as I untied the dinghy painter cleated to the rickety dock. A truck pulled up to her and stopped. I saw her talk briefly with the driver, then walk around and get inside the passenger side. I started my outboard and drove home, thinking about Marbella what life must be like for her.

While I had no desire to be a hooker, I found it fascinating that others did. There were always women selling themselves but never admitting it, the type that do a thorough search for men with money then strut their wares and see if they can snag some *dinero* for easy work. But that's a whole other story having to do with community property states and the marriage-minded.

As weeks would become months, I periodically ran into Marbella in town in the late afternoon and early evening, as I still basically kept sane hours in town. Then I got a job at Fred's Disco on Saturday nights. The band started at 8:30 p.m. and usually finished just before midnight. After cleaning up and settling up with Fred and such, I would find myself on the streets walking home late at night. Whenever I saw Marbella, we would stop and chitchat.

I admired her clothes, very fancy and form fitting, but nothing I would ever wear. She admired my various sarongs, as was my custom of the time, things she would never wear either. Sometimes she wore high heels, which gave her hips a bit more fullness and a swing to her walk. Sometimes people who knew her profession stared at me, wondering if I was one too. But I ignored them because I wasn't a lady of the night. I saw nothing being wrong with friendship with a prostitute. She never told me about her work; we mainly discussed outfits and the weather and how we felt that day or evening. Sometimes she would stop by Fred's on Saturday nights when I worked there.

She liked to drink scotch straight up, chased by a water back. She'd lean seductively up against the bar and scan the crowd with her dark brown, round eyes. People always noticed her perfect body and form-fitting dresses. Her legs were bare but shaved smoothly, and she might wear sandals or very high heels. Her plain face was decorated only with bright plum lipstick. Then one day I quit running into her. For months I wondered what had become of her. Was she taking a much needed and desired vacation from her profession? Had she met an untoward end as sometimes happens in this sort of profession? Or had she simply moved on, as many in her lot do?

Months went by, and one day I traveled to another island to buy a jeep. I needed to put it on a ferry back to St John, where I would use it in my new business. So I went over early to make the transaction and spend the day shopping and running errands on St Thomas. As I drove my new trusty rusty red heap of a jeep down Veterans Drive on the waterfront heading toward Charlotte Amalie, I was surprised to see a familiar figure up ahead on the left sidewalk. So I honked and slowed down. Marbella turned, expecting another customer. It had been well over a year since we had seen each other.

"Marbella, want a ride?" And instantly I did indeed feel like a customer, though this was not the intent. Marbella smiled and strolled around to the passenger side. Even though we drive on the left, all our cars are left-hand drive, just like in the states. Cars backed up behind me, islanders are usually fairly tolerant of those who stop to give someone a ride. She got in the jeep, and I asked how she was doing.

"Just fine," she said. "You live in St Thomas now?"

"No, I just came over to buy this jeep. I'll put it on the last ferry tonight and take it to St John. You living over here now? Haven't seen you in ages."

"Yeah, I came over here. I liked living in St John better, but the money just isn't there anymore. Not with all the crack heads. See, I don't do drugs, just a little drink here and there—well you know that, you served me Scotch at Fred's all the time. Sometimes I like to smoke a joint, but not that often. And crack and cocaine I stay away from, but it is everywhere these days, it seems. I just couldn't compete anymore."

I mulled this over, wondering just how many prostitutes could a tiny island like St John support? There were supposedly only about four to five thousand residents, and since many did not engage the services of a hooker, that left a small percentage who might. Sex can be fairly casual in the islands; people seem to sleep around more freely than in the states. Or maybe it is just that people tend to know each other's business more and who is sleeping with whom. Everyone knows who likes to sleep around a lot and who runs through lovers rapidly. St John was indeed a small and gossipy place where one could not go unnoticed for long. But in St Thomas, in sharp contrast, one could be relatively invisible, just another face in the population of forty or fifty thousand.

The census couldn't get an accurate check. People moving in and out almost daily, the numbers swelling the winter months and thinning in the summer months. The constant blur of tourists coming and going. Plus many anonymous people, often living under an assumed name, working for cash-only jobs to maintain even more obscurity, manufacturing stories about their past or refusing to acknowledge them at all.

Occasionally, someone would be picked up and the shocking details printed in the newspaper. How they were wanted for something hideous on the mainland or some foreign country. People would get drunk and tell you they were six years behind on child support for four kids somewhere. Or wanted for questioning about a robbery they had nothing to do with, but knew who did, or so they claimed. Amazing the secrets I eventually found out from talking with people. People like this did everything possible to keep their names off any lists, or if forced to put their name somewhere, may invent a whole new one.

Maybe Marbella sensed my questioning thoughts about the number of prostitutes actually working in St John. She went on to explain.

"Those crack-heads, Katrina and Lydia. They been giving blow jobs for five dollars. I can't get twenty-five dollars when they be giving head for only five dollars. And last week, Katrina was so desperate for a fix, that she was soliciting blow jobs for three dollars."

"You're kidding!" I gasped in mock horror. Frankly I'd never had a conversation about sexual practices and their costs. I found the conversation embarrassing, yet at the same time fascinating.

"Right there in front of the Lutheran Church at the four corners, across from the bank and the communications center. At three in the afternoon, no less. I seen and heard she myself, she stopping every man that come by. Father Ken came by and she nearly ask he before she finally remember who he is."

I winced a little at the improper use of "she" and "he" but this was a common West Indian trait. Sometimes I even found myself lapsing into the local lingo myself, especially when dealing with other West Indians—and sometimes to shock the continentals that flock the islands and never once talk with a West Indian unless expressly forced to, such as when dealing with the bureaucrats.

Father Ken, now that brought back fond memories, just the mention of his name.

I thought of my passenger and her openness at revealing the cost of blowjobs on St John. We drove on a few minutes in silence and then she waved and hollered at someone in a green Buick from the opposite direction. She asked me to let her out and I stopped the jeep in the middle of traffic, a common driving trait in the islands. She hopped out, and the oncoming traffic stopped; she dashed across the street and then disappeared into the green Buick.

I haven't seen Marbella since. I hope she is happy and doing well wherever she is.

Pirates in Paradise

Writer's note: So as not to embarrass the innocent franchise nor insult the island, their names have been changed to protect their piracy—oops, excuse me, I mean, to protect their privacy.

There are many freebooters in paradise. This was aptly demonstrated the years that Virgin Burger chose to invade the island with their fast-food chain. I wonder if they ever realized that piracy is still alive and well in the Caribbean. Perhaps it is not as readily noticed as it appears in its more subtle forms these days. For instance, the big hamburger chain decided that since Lusty Island sported no franchised fast-food restaurants, they would venture in and do very well there. The island was part of the U.S. territory and naturally attracted many Americans. The chain perceived little competition from the other restaurants; Virgin Burger would be the only franchised fast food.

What the executives never thought to figure into their cost-benefit analysis was the sheer competition from their customers as they surreptitiously fought to steal the chain's profits. This phenomenon was to puzzle the CEO's right up until they considered the idea of closing the place down. For the first time in Virgin Burger history, they met defeat. Their company had never been forced to close a location. Not ever. Sure, occasionally, they had moved around the neighborhood, securing a better lease, but once Virgin Burger chose an area to open, it remained an icon. Such was the company's past history.

With great expectations, Virgin Burgers opened in a lovely seaside mall that sported open-air hallways and offered a spectacular view of the shimmering Caribbean Sea. The residents and tourists flocked to the familiar franchise. They savored the more-or-less quick burgers with fries, the chili, and the salad bar. Rumor was that it quickly soared to the number one place in sales for all the Virgin Burger restaurants, including the numerous ones dotting the landscape of America's mainland. Soon that rumor was augmented with rumblings that it also sported the *lowest* net profit of all. This naturally resulted in a long run of replaced managers.

While the management was handed over from one promising manager to the next, the employees also went through rapid turnover. The CEO's had strict policies about missing work. Here in the islands, on a good surf day, the surfers wouldn't show for work. If Foxy's was having a big party, half the sailors had to take time off work to go. It was sheer madness trying to write an employee schedule. For the most part, the employees seemed to take the schedule as a slight hint as to the hours they should show up. They traded shifts amongst themselves, and the hapless manager might find his shift woefully understaffed or grossly overstaffed, rarely resembling the posted employee schedule.

Such was life at Virgin Burgers. A high turnover in employees was not uncommon for the franchise, but generally they were able to attract and train a few good mangers and rely on them to deal with the constantly changing staff. The higher-ups just didn't realize that the manager had to deal with multiple complexities with the employees on Lusty Island. Most didn't have cars, which meant they walked or hitchhiked to work. To complicate things, child-care is a hit and miss situation in the islands where there are an abundance of single parents. So on holidays and such, parents were likely to have their kids in the restaurant, eating or playing or running amuck, while they worked overtime. When Election Day rolled around, the employees informed the manager they got a half-day off to go vote, so they all cut their shifts in half and left; some in the evenings, when the polls were long closed.

As the discerning reader can perceive, the CEO's in Timbuktu obviously failed to take into account the nature of the culture where they were running their new restaurant.

The cost of living is very high on Lusty Island, but often wages are very low. The island comes under the U.S. minimum wage laws, and that is exactly what Virgin Burger paid most of the employees. The employees, in turn, compensated for this by helping themselves and their families to a bit of food from time to time.

In addition to what the employees took, the clientele also figured out divergent ways of beating the system. I believe if Virgin Burger had taken stock of their ratio of coffee to sugar packets, they might have realized for every cup of coffee sold, a hundred packets of sweetener vanished. Patrons, seeing the high cost of food in the island, were only too happy to stuff their purses, bags and pockets with sugar and sweetener packets for home consumption. If one managed to visit Virgin Burger once a week, one could probably steal enough sugar and Sweet and Low to last a week or more. Boaters also found this convenient.

Of course there were also the ketchup packets, which the employees were instructed to hand out meagerly. But that did not stop people from demanding a bunch of ketchup, often through a slight bit of intimidation. Such as squeaking one's teeth loudly, proclaiming, "Dat's all de catsup you can give me for d'ese fries mon?" (More teeth squeaking.) "Come on, now, d'ese packets so tiny, give me a handful!"

Virgin Burger probably thought it was perfectly safe to have self-service napkins. They were wrong, but they seemed not to notice the alarming rate at which these emptied out. The employees had to refill these contraptions hourly, if not sooner. Almost any boat or house you dined in sported the familiar trademark yellow napkins. By shopping at Virgin Burger, one could easily trim a good bit off of the family food budget, thanks to the innocent generosity of the chain's methods.

Then there was the tea scam. Virgin Burger offers free tea refills. No big deal you think, tea is cheap, how much can one person consume in a given meal? Well, they did not figure in two things: one, their store layout; and two, the nuts that routinely inhabit Lusty Island. You see there was a front door, which opened off an open breezeway from the mall. Then there was a side door, which opened to an outdoor deck with umbrella-covered tables for the patrons. This deck, in turn, opened out onto the beach. Virgin Burger figured that since everything was paid at the time of purchase, there was no need to worry about those who wondered in and out of the place. But a few enterprising folks figured out the tea scam right away. What they would do is buy one ice tea. Of course when they wanted a refill, they would take it back and politely ask for one. As the employees were instructed, they handed it over cheerfully. What they did not recognize was just *how old* that paper cup was. Some customers carefully kept their Virgin Burger cup for *weeks,* gaining free refills every day while on the beach.

Some kindly unsuspecting employees often looked at the shabby cup, tossed it in the trash and issued a new cup to the patron for their refill. It was like Russian roulette with the Russians in your favor. Occasionally a cup might fall apart or accidentally get tossed, then the hapless customer was forced to finally fork over money for a new tea, receiving the trademark cup for endless refills over the life of the cup. The coffee drinkers repeated this same scan, though I don't believe it was quite as frequent. Old coffee cups are somewhat more disgusting in appearance than old cups that have held iced tea.

Perhaps enormous losses of tea, sugar, ketchup, and napkins wouldn't have brought the hamburger giant to her knees, but the salad bar could have. Okay, those at the top figured salad bars are cheap; most folks that eat at them are dieting anyhow, others just turning to a healthier lifestyle, and it answered the vegetarians' needs. A certain father and daughter figured out how to beat the salad bar. Once others discovered their method, they often adopted it, adding a creative touch to the variety of thefts.

In the case of the father and daughter, he'd leave the little girl to sit on the deck innocently awaiting her daddy. He would go inside, order and pay for one iced tea and one salad bar. This would be handed to him on a plastic tray with a plastic plate and fork. He would then fill up his salad plate, meet his daughter with two straws to share their tea. Next, he'd dump his salad onto the plastic tray, and then send his daughter in to fill up the now-empty plate for herself. She would also tell the clerk she dropped her fork and fetch one for herself. Thus two could eat for the price of one.

Virgin Burger saw no need to watch the deck; they figured whoever was sitting out there had prepaid for their food, so they never saw the little scams like this. Many couples enjoyed a cheap date this way. The salad bar appeared to be a booming success, but here again, had they figured the ratio of pounds of salad per sales of salad bar, they might have figured that something was amiss. Or else Lusty Island had the hungriest salad-loving people in the world.

Another trick was the easy stir-fry dinner. Virgin Burger's salad bar carried a nice assortment of precut veggies, as well as nuts and seeds. One could request a salad bar to go. Then take the to-go box and cram it with all the veggies and nuts that would fit into it, and more. These were then taken home and with a little oil and meat, turned into a stir-fry for six. To get even more veggies, some people preferred the old Styrofoam to-go swap. Styrofoam to-go boxes are sold in many grocery stores on the island. Some found it advantageous to buy the empty boxes and then cruise through the salad bar during a crowded lunch hour, filling all their boxes while appearing to have paid for the salads.

Others preferred to do this in tandem. One person would go in and purchase a salad bar to go. After filling their box, they would linger at the condiments counter, pretending to select salt and pepper or napkins. Another friend would dash in with an empty to-go box in hand and merrily greet their friend, setting their box on the counter. As they chatted and agreed to meet on the beach for lunch, the visitor would grab the already full salad box and head out the door. The paying customer then would wander back to the salad box with empty box in hand and fill it up for free, with paid receipt in hand.

I even heard of a couple who used to take their salad plates home from Virgin Burger, the not-to-go type, but the little oval plastic ones they issued for dining in the restaurant. Then they would wash these for a later visit to Virgin Burger. Approaching from the deck side, they would choose a table and surreptitiously pull out their washed plates and ease them onto the table before them. One-by-one, each would sneak into Virgin Burger side door, amble over to the salad bar and help themselves.

The employees would, just before closing, "accidentally" cook up a huge batch of French fries. Realizing their apparent gaff, and not being able to save the French fries for the next day, they gleefully packed them up and took them home to their families along with the odd burgers that they could sneak out. Sneaking out burgers became easy. Throughout the evenings several burger orders would be processed "wrong." So the burger would be remade and the other one set aside, presumably to be tossed in the trash, but in reality tossed into an employee's bag. This was the land of new technology and most had microwaves at home. Even so, a cold free burger was often preferable to a hot burger that wasn't free.

Once the managers assigned an employee to maintain the salad bar. Her job was to clean up the inevitable messes people make at public salad bars, as well as restock. She was a lazy sort, so she used to stand near the salad bar and bark at the customers, "Don't make a mess!" (Squeaking her teeth.) "You people come in and make such a big mess." (Squeaking teeth again.) "I ain't cleaning up after you!" (Squeaking teeth.) "Hey, you spilling something! Stop that now!" (Squeaking teeth.)

Eventually, due to her poor customer relations, she was let go. After that, the odd employee would pop out of the kitchen, check the salad bar, straighten it up, add a few things, and then go back to the kitchen.

The executives in Timbuktu must have been scratching their heads. How could this place be their number one seller, yet have such a poor net profit? The wages were the same as in the U.S., minimum. The food was slightly higher, what with shipping costs, but then they had the freedom to charge slightly higher than their mainland counterparts. Plus, they bought in such huge volume; they would send down large shipping containers with the Virgin Burger products.

One week would be frozen meats and fries, the next would be refrigerated products for the salad bar and condiments; another week, the dry container would have the canned goods, napkins and such. Sometimes the shipments came in on time and sometimes not. This did not affect the dry goods or the frozen goods, assuming the compressor kept working, but the refrigerated goods could arrive late and be near disaster as rotten tomatoes and wilted lettuce arrived. So the managers of the local Virgin Burger, having no explanation for the high cost of goods in relation to the sales, would blame it all on late shipments or shipments held up by customs. The wilted produce would have to be thrown out and replaced at local prices if the shipper could not get there in time to replace the other one.

The longer the burger joint stayed open, the more creative the local opportunists became. Since gossiping is a favorite pastime in Lusty Island, some shared their secrets with others, and the epidemic perpetuated. Others, like myself, quietly observed all this while lingering over lunch leisurely and watching these various scams pulled off.

The local police couldn't catch the crack dealers that operated less than a block from their air-conditioned precinct. They really weren't about to concern themselves with catsup thieves. So over several years, the Virgin Burger managers came and went, mostly mainland boys trained up there. They, too, knew nothing of the local customs or the environment they were coming into. They were just grateful to be in the sunny Caribbean. To them running one store or another was all the same, or so they thought. But as their net profits plummeted, they too hung on for dear life 'til the next replacement came in.

At one point, someone finally promoted a local as manager. Now, he well knew the little bits of theft going on, but figured it wasn't worth his time to consider; he was just giddy with the power of having Virgin Burger under his control and he had great fun dressing up for the job and being cheerful all day, ignoring the customers that might sneak out some sugar. He knew just how to juggle the work schedules, and the turn-over slowed down somewhat, but the food costs continued to soar.

In Timbuktu, the executives really began to worry. The lease was coming due and the mall now wanted a greedy increase, reasoning that, after all, Virgin Burger was packed with customers all the time and must be raking in the money. There was talk of admitting failure and shutting the place down. The reason for the lack of profit was never quite determined in Timbuktu, but the place on Lusty Island just could not seem to net a decent profit. The food costs were growing at a geometric rate against the increase in sales. Not a single manager had been able to change the tide. It was baffling.

One enterprising manger, disgruntled with the long hours, low pay, pressure from the top, and high cost of living on the tiny island, heard a delicious rumor. Apparently, the bureaucratic Health Inspectors were in town and they were not at all happy. Word on the street was they were quite grumpy. In one restaurant, the inspectors stood at the refrigerator with door wide open, supposedly inspecting the food. After a few minutes, they measured the temperature, declared the refrigerator too hot, and destroyed the food.

Another restaurant was in an uproar because an expensive shipment of shrimp had just arrived. With a sickening *splash*, the shrimp was ruined as the nasty inspector dumped bleach all over it. This was, of course, quite vicious, but for whatever reason, the inspectors seemed to target certain restaurants that day and ruin their inventory.

The manager of Virgin Burger tried to make sure his kitchen was up to standards. Luckily, he had freshly cleaned tile floors, gleaming stainless steel appliances, and even a clean grease trap. His goods were stored properly, the refrigerators and freezers at their correct temperatures, and for good measure, he set the thermostats as low as possible in case the inspectors tried to pull the same old trick.

Eventually, the inspectors made their way through town, and when they reached Virgin Burger they found a born-here local managing the place. Immediately, they relaxed; could be some kid with local connections, best not to upset him. They found nothing wrong with the kitchen and gave him a letter of approval.

The manager was quite relieved, but then, on an after-thought, he loaded up much of the frozen goods in garbage bags and hauled them out the back door, supposedly to go to the dump, but stashed them in his car. Then he wrote a report to the head office, telling them the inspectors had arrived and destroyed half the food after staring into the freezers long enough to bring the temperature above the legal limit. After all this idiocy, was reported the following week in the newspapers who thoughtfully did not mention any restaurant names, as the owners feared worse retaliation.

The executives sighed; they *must* either turn the profits around or else consider closing up. The manager heard rumbles of the imminent closure. He sent to the executives the letter of approval from the health department, assuring them that everything was *now* under control.

So, late one night, knowing that the manager would qualify for the generous unemployment benefits as well as sympathetic new employers should the place perish rather than close up due to net profit failure, he set his own plan in action. He had no idea that the home office would be eternally grateful for what they assumed was a fortuitous act of nature.

He sent all the staff home at closing and pretended to lock-up. Then he rearranged all the paper goods to be strewed around the hot vats of grease, which were supposed to be shut off and cooling. He turned the temperature up as high as possible, and then he shut off the water to the restaurant and the sprinkler system. Even though he had automatic fire extinguishers over the greasy vats, he managed to discharge them in another part of the kitchen, and then put them back in their place. Just before shutting the door, he stacked a box of napkins on a lighted grill.

He locked up the restaurant tightly and drove home. The next morning, the town was shocked that Virgin Burger had burned nearly to the ground. The fire department, all of three blocks away, was engrossed in an avid domino game when the call came in. Not accustomed to fighting fires very often, they were a bit slow getting ready and to the scene. Knowing there were safety extinguishers over the gas grills and deep fat fryers, they felt their lateness would not be noticed. The fire department arrived; they remembered the water truck but forgot the pump. Eventually they more or less put the fire out, saving the rest of the mall, but Virgin Burger was virtually destroyed.

The executives in Timbuktu were perplexed but delighted. The insurance policy covered things nicely; it was a total loss. With sympathies from the community, the staff was able to collect unemployment benefits or easily get work elsewhere; and in many cases both, due to the large cash-only businesses on Lusty Island. Many of the privately owned restaurants on the island pay only in cash, so sometimes it is easy for pirates to double dip.

The past manager had already snuck out heaps of goods and had them stashed at his house before the fire. His best friend in turn owned a small café and you can bet where all the Virgin Burger inventory ended up that week.

Ah, yes the life in paradise... with pirates.

◉◉

I have a notion that gamblers are as happy as most people, being always excited; women, wine, fame, the table, even ambition, sate now and then, but every turn of the card and cast of the dice keeps the gambler alive–besides one can game ten times longer than one can do any thing else

Lord Byron (1788–1824) British poet.

One should always play fair when one has the winning cards.

Oscar Wilde (1854–1900) Irish poet and dramatist.

Sometimes nothing can be a real cool hand.

From the movie "Cool Hand Luke"

Money won is twice as sweet as money earned.

From the movie "The Color Of Money"

The Regulars

Mickey, Sol, Derrick, and I sat at the poker table, and a mild tropical breeze filtered through the smoke of too many cigarettes. We four were gathered for our weekly game of poker at the Pink Papaya Pub & Grub. We were waiting for the arrival of a fifth player, wondering who it would be. As Derrick would often say, they're the *boyz* and I'm the *gull*. At first the boyz found it odd that a poker-playing *gull* would strive to become a regular at their weekly game. But I was worthy, although at first I took a lot of their money with my inane bimbo tricks.

I still remember that first night when they fell for every one of them. On the third hand I asked ever so innocently, "Excuse me, but is four of a kind better than two pairs?" This caused everyone to fold, and I took the hand with only a pair of threes.

On another round where I was feigning ignorance, we were playing five-card draw. When my turn came around I asked, "Do I *have* to trade any cards?" When told no by a surprised dealer, I hemmed and hawed and reluctantly turned loose of only one card. Two players folded and the other two eyed me suspiciously. I raised the pot outrageously and one more folded. I raised it again, causing the last contestant to fold. I managed to take the pot with a King high, having only four hearts and wishing for the fifth, which of course I did not get on my draw. After that the boyz realized they might be in trouble.

While I cleaned them out to the tune of over seven hundred dollars that first night, we still garnered respect for each other and they welcomed me as a kindred spirit. Within a few weeks, we became tight friends. Other than poker, we did not have much in common with each other. We were of different nationalities, various ages, and diverse social standing. Somehow, our weekly poker games overcame all that, and we had a refined understanding established as the weeks and years rolled by and the poker games continued.

Now I was an established player, yet a novelty whenever a new player joined us. The macho idea that poker is *for-men-only* still permeates the male brain to this day. A newcomer might join us for the entire night or for only a few hands. Either way, we expertly cleaned them out as they mournfully came to the realization that we had been around the block a time or two and were not as dumb as we might look and act.

Mickey, our poker host and owner of the infamous Pink Papaya Pub & Grub, wore an enormous straw-hat, slightly tattered at the edges where Julian had gnawed on it. Julian is our talking parrot. The expansive straw-hat perched artistically on Mickey's distinctive head balanced out his massive frame and dwarfed Julian. Mickey's shaggy beard and long dark hair overhanging his shoulders hadn't seen a prune in years. He always sat at the west end of the immense poker table. An imposing person with a keen wit and an infectious chuckle, his huge frame filled out the wooden corner bench built into the wall as his belly gyrated up to the table's edge. Mickey could no longer fit into an ordinary bar chair, hence on the last round of remodeling, a custom bench, very sturdy indeed, had been built to accommodate his bulky physique. When Mickey laughed, which was often, his flabby belly would jiggle with giggles.

One night while we were playing, a small earthquake, so common in the Caribbean, shook and rattled the old rickety building. We all looked at each other in stunned silence while the tremors subsided. We speculated as to whether it was an earthquake or if Montserrat's Soufriere Hills volcano had finally blown. After a brief discussion, we settled on an earthquake and dealt the next hand. (Later it was reported to be an earthquake of 4.7 on the Richter scale.)

Then Mickey cracked up at another dumb-blond joke, my latest, (the guys loved it that I brought dumb-blond jokes to the game).

How do you get a blond to marry you?

Tell her she's pregnant.

Mickey thought this hilarious and his belly once again went into all sorts of gyrations as he whooped and giggled. Seeing this, a wry poker player remarked, "My God, it's another earthquake!" We nearly killed ourselves trying not to fall out of our chairs. Mickey, good-natured about the joke at his expense, laughed all that much harder.

Julian the parrot used to come to the Pink Papaya Pub & Grub for daycare only. His owner, a form-carpenter, would drop him off in the morning on his way to work (while picking up an icy-cold beer-to-go, breakfast of champions). He'd usually retrieve Julian in the afternoon or late evening. He might spend the night drinking while Julian ate peanuts. Then he'd put Julian on his drunken shoulder and stumble his way home with him.

Five months ago, Julian's owner had gone to the States for a one-week vacation. Though originally from the mainland, he had not been there in nine years. So, Julian was parked at the Pink Papaya Pub & Grub for the week. Julian's owner, upon landing in Miami on an early morning flight, rented a car and stopped for breakfast.

After tanking up with his usual beer and driving away, he apparently failed to remember that, whereas we islanders drive on the *left* side of the road, the U.S. still drives on the right-hand side. Julian's owner plowed down the wrong interstate ramp and into a fatal head-on-collision. Though his family sent for his belongings and photo albums, no one sent for Julian (there being problems with Julian's traveling documents, to boot). Apparently Julian had never been properly imported and therefore couldn't be legally relocated across dotted borders.

So Julian now lives on at the Pink Papaya Pub & Grub full-time, ascending the rafters and strutting up and down the bar. He loves old French bread for breakfast and peanuts for dinner. He likes to prattle and his preferred word is Julian-Julian. He also likes to perch on your shoulder and poop down your back and will nibble on your jewelry or hat if he's feeling jaunty. He is fond of cigarette lighters and if one is left on the bar, he will pick it up with his beak and waddle away with it.

Although we never taught Julian poker, he is a quick study. Sometimes in the middle of a heated game, Julian would yell out, "Cheat! Cheat!" While it startled some players, the rest of us would nearly fall out of our chairs with laughter. It never failed to alarm the other patrons of the Pink Papaya Pub & Grub and added a bit of much needed levity to the games. Another favorite was to screech, "Fold! Fold!" at the top of his tiny lungs. Mickey would yell, "Be quiet Julian! You're going to blow my hand!" While the bar customers were sure we had lost our minds for good, the rest of us would chime in, "Fold! Fold!" which kept Julian repeating the same thing.

Another of Julian's favorite words was "Brrrrriiiiing, brrrrriiiiig!" as he strained to imitate the incessant ringing of the bar phone. When someone would finally pick up the receiver, Julian would sing out, "Hello? Hello?" He said everything at least twice, if he dared to speak at all. Some days Julian could not be coaxed into saying a thing. One time, after Julian had his first chew on Mickey's latest straw hat, Mickey had yelled at him "Bad bird! Bad bird!" For the next two days, that's all Julian would say.

One could usually find Mickey and Julian, day or night, holding court at the poker table. The table served as Mickey's office because he didn't care to hunker in small rooms composing checks (and/or excuses) to suppliers. So he sat at the big table in the rear of the club with Julian usually nearby.

Tonight, I had arrived an hour early. Early arrivals were expected to clean up the poker table and set the game up along with its accouterments. Mickey may have been the host, but we were definitely the set-up crew. I made my way past the throng of happy-hour revelers, speaking to all of them (having seen them here many times before). Finally I was able to reach the back deck. There sat Mickey at the poker table.

"How ya' doing, sweetheart?" he caroled as he tipped his straw hat with his left hand.

"Hiya Mickey. I'm doing just fine. Can't complain, and can't find anyone to listen to me if I did."

"Huh! Look, you mind if I go catch a nap before the poker game? Just wake me up when you're ready."

"Sure, no problem. I'll get this..." as I eyed the scene before me.

Scattered about the table were three over-flowing ashtrays advertising various beers, two packs of crumpled cigarettes, a pile of Julian's stolen lighters, the club's scruffy phone book and the antique phone on three legs that wobbled when you dialed, a well-thumbed rolodex, four marinating drinks, a sullied coffee cup, five odd dirty dishes, today's paper (turned to a half-inked crossword), several crumpled up paid and unpaid bills, two paperbacks (one missing its cover), a foreign envelope addressed to a long departed bartender, a box of imported cigars, and two decks of cards. Amidst it all perched Julian, munching away on his peanut supper, making another little mess.

Mickey shuffled off to the club's office. There sat an old immense executive-size oak desk. Mickey discovered a Queen size mattress fit its top perfectly, so he had converted the desk to his living quarters. He kept his clothes and such in the drawers below and slept on top. The outside of the door had a neatly lettered sign that simply stated *Sorry, We Don't Cater To Persons In A Hurry (Same Day Service On **All** Orders)*. Mickey disappeared behind the door as I turned toward the bar and a well-deserved drink.

I grabbed an empty box from behind the counter and returned to the scene of the mess, taking a sip of my drink, a rum punch made with Cruzan dark. Then I began emptying the ashtrays and cleaning up the table. On the last bout of remodeling, Mickey had this immense oval table built. It was big, heavy, and made of mahogany. Mickey expressly built it for playing poker, but it became his outer-office shortly after completion.

Sitting in a niche on the rear deck of the club, an L-shaped bench gently curved around the western end and southern side. It could readily accommodate up to seven players, the most we ever played with. Mickey always sat at the west end of the table (to my left) and Sol presided over the east end (to my right). Though Sol and Mickey were twenty-five years apart in age, they often saw the world through the same lens.

On the other side of the table, three chairs fit neatly. Most nights we played with five players, and on busy nights we had six or seven with one or two spectators in the wings awaiting a chance to get on the table. It was ironic that the boyz assigned me the south side, as only me or maybe one other sat on my side if we had a full, seven players. Usually we started play with five, and I had the entire south side to myself.

I sorted through the debris scattered before me on the table. Some went in the garbage, while the dirty cups and dishes were reinstated to the bar and kitchen. I headed for a door marked with a professional sign that read: *Only Passengers With Tickets Beyond This Point.* Last year it was swiped when one of the Pink Papaya Pub & Grub regulars was hired to rebuild the airport after Hurricane Henrietta.

Joe had proudly marched into the club one night carrying his sign-trophy under one arm. He held a cordless drill and four screws in the other hand.

"Hey, Mickey!" he yelled half way across the club, "I brought you something. I'm gonna put it up now." With that he held the sign to the kitchen door, retrieved a pencil from behind his ear, marked the four holes, drilled them out, then screwed the sign in place. He stood back to smile and admire his handy work. The sign was crooked.

"Ah, shiiittt..."

"Rut-Row!" said Mickey as he struggled to get out of his seat and come see what all this drilling was about. From his location, he couldn't quite see the kitchen door. Thump, thump, thump and the floor shook a little as Mickey made a few steps across the wooden deck so he could view the kitchen door around the corner.

He burst out laughing. The chef came through the door wiping her hands on a dirty apron.

"What's all this racket? I'm trying to make meat loaf in here!" She turned to look at the door and then went into peels of giggles. So there the sign stayed.

The new sign brought on a rash of surreptitious thievery, and within months the Pink Papaya Pub & Grub was sporting all types of signs and mislabeled doors. It seemed patrons wanted to out do each other with their pilfered sign-trophies.

Over the commode hung "20 Mile Speed Limit." Behind the bar, which was on the second-floor upper deck, was a window overlooking a lone papaya tree. Screen-less and glass-less, its heavy wooden shutters were thrown open each day. Above the window now hung a sign labeled *"Emergency Exit Only. An Alarm Will Sound."*

The storage room for excess inventory had a stolen ship's sign that read: *"DANGER. HIGH*

VOLTAGE" in six different languages including Greek, French, Spanish, German, and Swedish.

I walked through the "Passengers Only" door to the back of the kitchen and gossiped with the chef, who was lounging in a corner reading a book. I found the rusty can of furniture polish and a rag and went back out to dust and clean the table. The aerosol spit and sputtered. I shook it furiously and finally coaxed a bit of polish out of it. The Pink Papaya Pub & Grub was renown for its extreme casualness in regard to behaving as a business. It would never occur to any of the staff to give Mickey's table any service or to retrieve the various accouterments brought to him or departed by others who might dine or drink there, chatting with Mickey. Only on poker night did the table get any ministrations at all. Sometimes even then the bar and grill might be so short staffed that we'd be left to our own devices for even fetching our drinks. Customarily I did all the scurrying around if we didn't have a waitress or waiter. It didn't inconvenience me. I conducted my simple duties cheerfully and professionally. I liked playing poker with the boyz and I enjoyed fetching drinks for them between hands. Besides, I was the youngest in the group by at least ten years. (Age before beauty!)

After the table was polished, I retrieved ashtrays, coasters, cards and the chips. Sol strolled in, a pipe in hand. After exchanging pleasantries, he sat down to count out the chips in stacks of fifties. Derrick came in next and sat down, retrieving the wobbly phone from under the table. He dialed his wife and told her where he was, inquired about their son and then hung up. He put the phone back under the table. We were making inconsequential chitchat, exchanging gossip, promoting the coconut telegraph, and waiting for the table to be complete with five to seven eager contestants.

There were still the lights and fan to bother with and the magnitude of the movie volume blaring over the TV from the VCR. The Pink Papaya Pub & Grub was a bit chaotic at times. A band was setting up on the front lower deck. The bartender was playing her beloved tune at plenteous volume on the stereo.

Derrick clambered on a bar stool then the bar itself and re-arranged the spotlights, resetting the dimmer switch until Sol thought we had the most befitting light for poker. Somewhere a compromise between bright-enough-to-see yet dim-enough- to-lend-a-cloistered-aura, was achieved. It was getting dark outside and approaching our unofficial start time of sunset.

Depending on the prevailing breeze, the overhead fans might be slowed down or sped up. Due to scantiness of management, the excessive loudness of the TV was often the result of a debauched obstinate audience or self-righteous bartender. Neither had an intimation of what a *reasonable* volume was. Mickey would have to ultimately intervene and on poker playing nights, he tried to keep the movie and stereo at a dull roar.

Though it was a breezy tropical club, the table was fortuitously placed in a corner on the upper covered deck. One side of the deck faced the ocean with only a half wall to keep the bar patrons from tumbling out and landing twenty feet below. We rarely had calamity with flying cards. Yet, once at the conclusion of an especially gusty evening, we found two cards on the floor and were thoroughly abashed, as we had no notion how long they had been there. (One hand or twenty?) Often I quietly counted the cards when my deal came around, to make sure we had 52.

Between hands we had a chance to order more drinks, make quick phone calls, or visit the *Executive Office*. (At least that's what the custom fancy golden sign posted on the restroom door intoned.) This is the Caribbean, no his and hers, just a one-seater for everyone, much to the surprise of inquiring tourists.

On this particular night, some shoot-em-up movie was doing its loudest best at creatively killing half the actors in Hollywood in the autographed style of modern American entertainment, brought to us courtesy of the VCR. Drunks were hootin' and hollerin' like observing death and destruction was the most unconstrained and enchanting commodity. (A morbid statement as to what some adjudge as entertainment.)

Derrick turned around and said, "Hey, could y'all cut it down a little?" and was totally ignored by those engrossed in their suds and video. So he got up and walked over to Mickey's door and banged on it. Mickey, still in bed on the desk, threw open the door. Above the bed hung a sign *Parking For Parish Priest Only* (nabbed from the Catholic church late one night on a dare by two drunks).

Derrick burst out laughing, as he had not seen the new sign yet.

"Come on, Mickey. Let's play poker. Come out here and do something about this gawd-awful racket" and he waved at the TV behind him. Mickey rolled out of bed, straightened his T-shirt and wiped his brow, then lunged across the deck and sat heavily at the head of the table. He reached beneath the table and retrieved the remote control. Aiming it at the graphic volume, he toned it down to something more reasonable. This, of course, was met with groans from the movie watchers.

I took my seat at the table. Sol was still counting and arranging the chips. I could see the numbers tattooed on his arm. He was just a teenager during the awful Holocaust. How he survived is anyone's guess. I hadn't the heart to ask, and he had never said. He is such a charming gentle person. Every time I see that tattoo, I think of what an appalling childhood he must of had. I wondered if he had any family left, or was it just him now. Sol is probably the best player we have. He apparently has a phenomenal memory, as he seems to know every card and the odds of which card will turn up next. He often goes home the winner. Once I discovered he was the same age as my father. Though we never discussed it, I thought it odd that he and my father would have been in the same places at the same times when they were both barely 17. A war half a century ago and a world apart.

Derrick sat back down to Mickey's left, across from me. Derrick is very clean cut and has the olive good looks of a Lebanese, but an accent very New Yorkish, lately of Miami, by way of Chicago and now back living on our tiny island. He is a funny man indeed, seeing absurdity and humor in most everything. We haven't a clue where he gets his money. (He claims to have an export/import business but none of us know where this is or when he works at it.) His exotic wife vanishes periodically on lengthy trips and this doesn't seem to rattle Derrick in the least.

Derrick always arrives on time. He calls us if he's not going to be his usual prompt self. He's fun to play with and very skilled, and he's been known to suddenly drive the pot very high when he thinks he has a good hand. I can tell something about what he's holding by the degree to which he wrinkles up his forehead in serious consideration. Sometimes his playing is punctuated with visits by his son or wife or both or phone calls to and from.

When his wife was off-island for several months, Derrick brought his son with him. Every week, he arrived with Derrick and sat down at another table to watch the TV (habitually blaring some inappropriate movie). The youngster loved to hang out, eat a burger, watch us and watch the TV, and was well behaved because he liked the idea of telling his school mates that he hung out in a bar (drinking Shirley Temples) while his daddy played poker.

Derrick's boy is the reason we changed our Monday night game to Friday nights. The child could stay out later and not have to be up early for school, and so his dad could stay out late as well. We're a democratic kind of group. We modified the poker day to accommodate child-care needs.

When Derrick's wife finally returned to the island, she sometimes hung out in the club but pretty much ignored the poker game. The kid didn't get to stay out late much anymore. But Derrick's good-natured wife didn't mind Derrick staying out late with us. She knew us all and knew we were his closest friends, but she also saw to it that their young son went home at a more reasonable hour (and saw a lot less trash on the TV).

"Anyone call Milford?" intoned Derrick as he rearranged his cigarettes, ashtray, coaster and drink. Derrick had a habit of shuffling his accouterments endlessly until we dealt cards and his hands had something else to do.

Milford Cummings, the one-time, two-termed senator. He shows up irregularly and brings an abundant stake with him to start. He prefers a personal invitation by telephone. Each week. We rely upon his occasional presence at our poker games (and his former/current connections) to save us from the potential ire of cops.

Other than Milford's spacious family home, all of us players lived in small efficient housing (thanks to the outrageous rents charged in paradise!). Mickey lived in the former office at the club. Sol lived with his wife in a one-room apartment (the want-ads lovingly referred to as a *studio*) above a diner on the edge of town. Derrick and his family lived in a tight bungalow down an awful muddy road at the top of an outrageously steep mountain. I resided on a twenty-nine foot sailboat that possessed my entire worldly goods. Where else were we to play poker? At the Lutheran Church Hall?

Tonight Milford could be our fifth player and fill out our table. Since he had not yet arrived, Mickey was thumbing through the Rolodex. He grabbed the old phone from under the table, picked up the receiver and began dialing. The phone wobbled on its three legs as Mickey punched in the five-digit number. He was calling Milford to *invite* him. Milford was graciously flattered whenever someone called to *invite* him.

Milford loved to play poker with us, but preferred an invitation above the more common method of just showing up. Sometimes we would already assemble five players without having invited Milford yet. If Milford was out and about, he might drop in late and see if he could get in on the table. Sometimes he'd buy a player's chips and trade seats with them. For this, I was grateful to Milford. If I was winning and Milford should wander in late looking like he wanted to play, then I'd sell him my seat and chips. (Go home a winner!) It was important to me to try to go home a winner, even if it meant leaving early (not always an easy thing to do!). I was surviving off this poker money while I tried to pull myself together. I was living the life of a sea gypsy, looking for opportunities to pick up some money to support my habit—a craving sailboat that consumed every dollar I could scrounge.

Mickey got off the phone and said Milford was on his way. I got up to fetch a round of drinks for us all. Milford would probably show up within the next half-hour, immaculately dressed, as was his trademark style. He's 6'4" tall, incredibly dark with local family roots firmly planted and going back in time under all five flags this island has flown in its chaotic history.

Milford has mammoth hands that sport ponderous gold rings on each digit, accenting his expertly manicured fingernails. A heavy gold bracelet dangles on his right wrist and a Rolex gold watch on his left. The cards are dwarfed in his immense paws, their presence disguised by the dazzling array of jewelry. A slice of pizza is seen as a scant snack in his massive hand.

Once he shows up, you can doubtless guess he is good for the night; unless we should break him entirely, and then he makes a hasty exit. I think he brings around $1,000 or more a night to play. He notices, but doesn't seem to care, that I may show up the same night with only $50 (and play all night too!).

Milford has two ornate gold money-clips, custom made with his initials, bulging in large bills. One in each pocket. We surreptitiously learned that fact the night Milford lost awfully badly.

So, those are the regulars. And me of course. The *gull.* I'm just a sailor, cruising through on my endless stream of unsteady jobs. Sometimes we have a few others stop in and play on the fragmentary chance they might win it big.

Occasionally a tourist roaming through the bar will light up when they see us, and next thing you know they're asking how to get in on the game.

Once, a hefty red-faced man with a huge potbelly politely watched us play for a few minutes. Then he asked if he could join us, and we agreed. He asked how much the chips were worth and we said the whites are ones and the reds are five and the blues are tens.

"Dollars?" he croaked.

"Dollars."

"Oh, my, this is beyond me" and he embarrassingly got out of his seat and left the club.

We're polite to the newcomers; we explain the rules (rotating deal, dealer's choice of games, no wild cards, no loans, no guns, and a maximum of three raises). We're usually very patient. Though one night we had a drunk (whom we all knew), and he had begged to play. He misdealt and screwed up several of the games. He messed up his own hand. When we played jacks-or-better, he opened the game. He only had one jack instead of the required two. This messed us all up (a lone jack is nothing to bet on). But if he truly had had two jacks, well, that's a different story for opening in five-card draw. Finally someone said this was like playing *Monopoly rules* instead of poker! So we cleaned out the drunk's money and booted him out of his seat. We never let him play with us again.

Though we are used to the bar patrons standing around the table, we never let anyone sit at the table unless they are playing poker. Except Sol's wife. But that's different. She'll slip up quietly some nights and sit at the edge of the table corner to Sol's right. She'll watch a few hands, and then between hands she'll whisper something in Sol's ear, and then tell us all goodbye and leave. Once in a while she'll hang out at the bar if the movie looks good, but usually she just makes these ten-minute stops at the poker table then leaves again, never playing and never inquiring about Sol's winnings or losses. It's his money and his life and his friends. She's grateful to know exactly where he is and what he's doing (and with whom). In the thirty-eight years she has been married to Sol, she has never wanted for anything. Sol has always provided a modest comfortable life for her, a far cry from the squalor of poverty she grew up with.

He has never once asked her to account for the generous allowance he hands her each week for what he calls "wife-wants." Usually she sends most of it to her relatives and spends the rest on herself, getting her hair styled frequently and shopping for pretty clothes in bright colors. She couldn't care less if he wants to stay out every Friday night playing poker. A small concession for a generous man.

We poker players could be ruthless at times, and the only time I ever remember another *gull* playing with us was the new waitress. She had kept an eye on the table throughout the night as she worked around us. She thought we were having great fun (which we were!). Boisterous at times, we cut up a lot, since we're all good friends. We love to trade bad jokes, especially blond bad jokes (maybe because the sun has lightened my auburn hair to a near blond over the years?).

Later that night the waitress asked Mickey how late she should work. Since nobody was eating at that advanced hour, he told her she could take off. She asked to sit in on the poker game. Sure! We were eager for some fresh money on the table and quickly converted her eighty-two dollars in tips to poker chips.

We cleaned her out, taking all her tips in about ten minutes and three fast hands. She was flabbergasted. She stuttered, staring incredulously as Mickey raked in the last big pot, the one with the last of her chips.

"I need cab fare to go home."

"Looks like you're hitch-hiking," was the chilling reply. Poker is for keeps. "If you can't play for keeps, then don't play" is the unwritten, international poker-playing rule. You lay down your money, you take your chances, and you go home for better or for worse. Why she gambled her taxi fare on that last hand was anyone's wild guess. Poker makes people lose track of the value of money. Especially when it has been converted to little round plastic chips.

Tonight as we sat around the table, just the four of us waiting on a fifth player, probably Milford, Mickey asked me where I learned to play poker. So I began telling him about the Thursday-Night Regulars.

I took him fifteen years back and two thousand miles away to the Overbrook house where the Thursday-Night Regulars played nickel-dime-&-quarter poker. We always ordered pizza to be delivered. When the doorbell rang, whoever had the most money on the table had to buy it. That way, losers ate free and would maybe return another week to win or lose some more. The living room fireplace was often blazing in the chilly winter months we played.

Sometimes the doorbell would ring with near disastrous consequences. For example, one night this guy had been steadily losing. He was down to his last quarter and the pot was huge. And then boom! He won the pot after tossing in his last quarter. The doorbell rang as he raked in the pot, and by the time he paid for the pizza, he was practically broke again. We laughed and laughed over that one!

People showed up with coffee cans or zip locks or what-have-you full of change for the game. One guy used a Chivas Regal purple felt bag for his horde of change, and we were all envious. We didn't bother with chips, and our house rules were pretty lax. We sold change back and forth, so that we all more or less started with about equal stakes. We didn't do pennies. It was a fun and lighthearted game, though we played for keeps and always shared a pizza, paid for by the unlucky winner.

Our house rules were dealer's choice of game (wild cards acceptable), and then we would ante up. If you didn't like the game, you could leave the table and go poke the fireplace until the next one came up. The maximum bet was a dollar I think; gosh, it has been so many years since we played at the old oak table at Overbrook.

The table had a crack in the middle, and any money that fell through the crack belonged to the "house." Some weeks the house made upwards of two dollars or more.

I told Mickey and the crew about Gill, the blind player. Now you may wonder why we were playing poker with a blind man, or better yet *how* we were playing with a blind man. No, we never once cheated him either. It's not cool to cheat at poker. It's dangerous too. After all, people used to kill each other over suspected cheating in the days of the Wild Wild West.

Gill was barely thirty. The ravages of diabetes had claimed his eyesight about a year earlier.

Naturally, he was very depressed at this tremendous loss. Through a friend of a friend, he heard about our games. Gill loved to play cards, and he loved to play poker. So one night he caught a ride and ended up on my doorstep, asking to play cards with us. He had his own set of Braille playing cards, a bit tattered at the edges, as he had spent the last year learning to read them. Gill instantly became a Thursday-Night Regular. He also taught me many blonde jokes. (My favorite one was about two blondes who drove to Florida on vacation. When they got near Orlando, the sign said "Disney World Left" so they turned around and went home.)

We changed the rules some after Gill joined us, which made us more professional in our games. What we did was, as every card was dealt face up, it was called out loud so Gill could follow the action. All bets were made verbally as well and strictly in turn so Gill could always chime in when it got around to him. We admonished players who didn't follow these rules. At first Gill would get a bit confused and when his turn came around to bet or draw cards, we would sometimes have to reiterate the cards on the table and who was showing what where and what the pot was up to and so on.

Gill was incensed if anyone tried to touch or look at his cards, as new players didn't know how to react to a blind player and wanted to grab his hand away and whisper loudly what he had. But after a few weeks of our new routine, Gill was an old pro. We could deal out the cards, naming the face up ones as they were dealt and Gill would always know who had what and where, showing. We played with his Braille cards so he could read his own cards. He usually hid his cards beneath the table, but we allowed that as it was unlikely that anyone could sneak in another Braille card, the deck being very distinct. No one wanted him to deal. Everyone thought he'd know what the cards dealt face down were since he could finger them first and thereby read them. So when his deal came around, we let him choose the game and I'd deal it for him since I was the hostess. So after awhile it seemed entirely natural that we would play poker with a blind man every Thursday.

And the poker games helped pull Gill out of his awful depression.

After a few weeks, it was suggested we needed a new deck of cards. But as I pointed out, we needed Braille cards because of Gill. He promised to get a new set. We were wearing out his only deck as we all struggled to learn Braille, too. Most of us never got the hang of it, but it was a fun past time.

Gill's social worker got a huge laugh out of his request. He called her up to ask her where the cards had come from. Someone had given

By Dear Miss Mermaid

him the set once when he was in the hospital. She said, "You mean you need another deck already?"

Well, he explained about the weekly poker games, and she just roared. He countered with, "What else am I to do at night? Watch movies? Playing poker is fun, and the group is real nice." Plus, he pointed out that poker playing was improving his memory, a useful asset for a blind person.

Two weeks later Gill was sporting two brand new decks of cards, and the games went on. The pizza parlor knew us simply as "the Overbrook house." Week after week, year after year, we ordered our pizzas, poked the fireplace, and roared with laugher as we dealt hand after hand. One night we all smoked cigars. But the cat threw up and the drapes stank for weeks, so we never bothered with the cigars again.

My neighbor Richard used to drop in. He never once played poker, but liked to lean against the wall near the French doors that separated the living room and dining room and watch the players. He thought we were nuts. When he discovered Gill was blind, he *knew* we were nuts.

Richard never liked for *anything* to go on at my house without his knowledge. When cars started parking in front every Thursday night, he would stroll over to see who was there and what we were doing. Richard had grown up in a

strict household where cards were not allowed
nor was drinking or dancing. So Richard was
fascinated with this bit of evil. We got used to
having him stand there and watch us, and occasionally he would turn his attention to the fireplace in the living room and pick up the massive
fireplace poker. Then he'd poke the fire or add
a log. I liked fires in the winter and built one
first thing after work every Thursday. Sometimes
I'd come home to find my live-in lover, Stephan,
had already built a fire. He played poker too
when he wasn't booked to play music at the
nightclub.

I clearly remember the day I bought that
fireplace poker. I was at an arts and craft show
and a blacksmith had forged this beautiful tool
along with a decorative hook. It was massive and
functional. It hung to the right of the fireplace.
Everyone loved the heft of it. Human nature
being what it is, it is hard to resist poking the fire.
Then there's the add-a-log-routine and poke-
poke-poke until it is in the just-right place.

My sister Rita had arrived one evening. She
had a month-old baby, and her husband was out
of town. She came to stay with me and show off
her new baby. He was being breast-fed, and Rita
still wore maternity clothes because that way she
could slide the baby under her shirt for discreet
nursing. Well, it was Thursday night, and Rita
thought a poker game would be fun, having

never really played much before, but knowing the general rules. Stephan didn't have a music gig until Friday night, so he'd be playing poker too. He had built a lovely fire in the living room that morning to warm Rita and her baby while I was at the office.

Gill showed up at the same time I pulled in the driveway. My brother, Calvin, one of the regulars, came early to see his new nephew. So tonight we expected a lot of fun, and we already had five players one hour before the start of our game. We took turns cooing over the baby. Gill was holding him when he drifted off into baby-land sleep. Rita and I went into the guest bedroom and fashioned a crib out of a dresser drawer, padded with a pillow and a baby sheet. She carefully tucked his tiny body under the pastel blanket and we set the dresser drawer on the floor, next to the steam radiator. We cut off the lights and only half closed the bedroom door.

The fire was blazing as we lounged about the living room. We speculated whether or not anyone else would show up. Stephan said maybe Richard would come over to play. We all laughed 'cause Richard *never* played poker with us but chose to be our weekly spectator. Richard was a lonely man. He loved to come over and visit whenever he saw another car pull up in my driveway. He just *had* to know who was at my house. I always introduced him, yet he was a man of few words. We were used to Richard being a silent eyewitness to much of my social life at the Overbrook house. Richard was almost like a movable statue, silently surveying the unfolding scene.

Richard had met every man I ever dated, my entire family and all my friends. He was even there when Stephan moved in at the odd time of four in the morning and eventually became my live-in lover. Yet Richard rarely ever said anything. Just stood around watching us. After awhile he'd mumble something like, "Later, folks" and walk out the front door and go home. That was Richard, and we were used to him in our lives. Richard and I each thought the other eccentric and tolerated each other in an odd intimacy that was rarely consummated by conversation.

Occasionally Richard would ask something personal to clarify what he had seen. When we would try to question him, he answered often in a one-syllable answer, like a grunt. His way of saying he wasn't up to talking. Once he did ask me why Stephan moved in at four in the morning. After I told him, he nodded and then turned and walked out the door.

Stephan was a talented musician. Several months before, he had moved two hundred miles away to play at the beach for the summer. He managed to put himself into a fine jam with a young lady and decided after his gig one night to pack up and leave town. He drove two hundred miles through the night, his truck piled high with his sound equipment and luggage. The front passenger seat was filled with box after box of cassette tapes. At four in the morning he pulled in my driveway. We hadn't seen each other in the months since his move, nor had we talked in that period. We had never dated but were good friends. Close enough that he felt little nervousness ringing my doorbell. The dog reached the door first and barked her one-woof greeting, followed by a sleepy me.

Stephan sought refuge in my guest bedroom until he could find a permanent place to live locally again; he was finished at the beach for this season, anyway. I welcomed the company as I had been rambling around that big old house alone for years, save for my dog and cat. Stephan liked to putter around the house and fix various derelict things like the wiring or plumbing. He got a weekend gig at the Pitts Private Pub around the corner from us. Eventually Stephan found a permanent place to live and moved down the hallway to my bedroom, although that was not the original intent when he first appeared on my steps that fateful night. Somehow, Richard had woken up and strolled over at 4 a.m. and actually helped lug Stephan's musical gear into the house. No, Richard did not miss much that went on at my house.

Tonight after the start of the first poker hand, the baby started wailing in the next room where he was presumably sleeping. Rita retrieved the little fellow and stuck him under her shirt to nurse and sat back down to the poker game. The second hand was dealt. Richard chose this moment to come in the house. Richard never knocked or rang the bell. He just walked in. It was kind of odd, but that's just what he did. Not an uncommon act in a Southern neighborhood where you had grown up with the folks. But we hadn't grown up together, and everyone in the neighborhood was second and third generation home owners, it being mostly older homes being reclaimed by yuppies.

So in strolled Richard. He spoke and nodded, a man of few words, then went over and picked up the fireplace poker and played with the fire. When he was done, he leaned it to the left of the fireplace instead of hanging it up on its hook to the right of the fireplace where it belonged. This irritated me, but I decided not to mention it, preferring not to be niggling.

Richard then took up his favorite position; with arms folded across his chest, he casually leaned on the French door frame and watched the game in the dining room. His back was to the fireplace, which was about five feet away over his right shoulder on the adjacent wall.

Last time Richard had seen Rita, she was just starting to show her pregnancy. He apparently thought Rita was now very pregnant, due to her bloated maternity shirt. He hadn't a clue that a live baby was suckling contentedly under the safety and warmth of her shirt. I forgot it was news to Richard that the baby had been born last month. No one bothered to mention it as we were engrossed in our latest hand and the pot was now upwards of six dollars. As the third poker round ended, the baby apparently fell asleep. Rita decided to put him back to bed in his dresser drawer.

We took an informal break since it was between games. Calvin went to the bathroom. Stephan went to make drinks. I got up to order a pepperoni pizza to be delivered, using the phone in the hallway, and Gill kept his seat, his back to Richard.

Rita stood up from the poker table, one arm aiding the baby concealed beneath her bloused top. She reached under her shirt and plucked the sleeping child discreetly out from under her maternity top. She was concerned with her newborn child and not really paying attention to Richard at all. Like I said, he was just kind of a mobile statue, familiar to us all. But apparently, he was intently studying Rita's moves.

Boom! He fainted and fell backwards into the living room. His head crashed into the fireplace poker with an awful thud. His wide-open eyes were motionless, as big as saucers. A pool of blood rapidly formed around his head.

Rita screamed, Gill jumped out of his chair, I ran from the hallway, Calvin emerged from the bathroom, still zipping up his pants, and Steve came dashing in with a drink in each hand. The baby started crying, and we all gasped in horror as we stared at Richard. We had each heard the awful thud, yet none of us had actually seen Richard fall. A hasty explanation was made to Gill, and he slumped down in his chair. For once, he was grateful for his blindness, being spared the gruesome sight that greeted the rest of us. I ran for the linen closet, grabbed the first towels I saw and dashed back to the living room. I gingerly lifted up Richard's head to wrap the towels around it and was sickened to see that more than just blood was pouring out of him.

Stephan leapt for the hallway phone and hastily dialed 911 for an ambulance. I could hear him yelling at the top of his lungs, "We need an ambulance now! There's been a terrible accident! We need help! We're at 19 Overbrook Drive! We need an ambulance! Yes, I'll be standing in the street, just send them *now!* Oh, God, it's awful, I don't know if he's alive or not. Blood, there's blood everywhere. *Please,* we need help *now!*"

He then hung up the phone and yelled, "I'm going to flag them down!" And he tore open the front door and dashed out into the street. Then he ran back inside and turned on the porch lights and the security outdoor lights he had just installed the previous week. The yard was bathed in the eerie, yellow glow of the floodlights. He stood in the middle of the street; anxiously looking up and down as if the ambulance were there and he just couldn't make it out yet.

Momentarily, we heard the weak wailing of a distant ambulance. After what seemed like an eternity, the summoned ambulance arrived screaming in the night, flashing the whole neighborhood with its strobe. The attendants dashed in and one checked Richard's pulse. He looked knowingly at the other attendant and said, "We'd better go *now!*" They lifted Richard onto the stretcher, along with the soaked towels. They whisked him out and expertly loaded him in the back of the ambulance and took off, the siren shrieking in the night.

Every house in the neighborhood turned on their outdoor lights, and flocks of people came running out to see what all the commotion was about. We dashed back inside and closed the curtains and locked the door. Nobody was in the mood for neighborhood chitchat. Someone began pounding on the front door, demanding to know what was going on. I just wanted them to go away. It sounded like an angry throng was gathering in my front yard, so I went to the back door and let the dog outside. She ran around to the front of the house and chased everyone off the lawn, then settled down on the front porch to guard us. Occasionally we heard a low growl out of her and then retreating steps. We were all in shock and just couldn't deal with curious neighbors at that point.

I stared in horror at the living room floor and the unmentionable stuff attached to the business end of the poker. First I grabbed more towels and just covered up the whole mess. I was shaking all over. Rita was white as a ghost and seemed oblivious to the crying infant she cradled in her arms. Stephan was running around the house, a complete nervous wreck, and then he spied the two drinks he had made for Gill and himself. He gulped the first one down in about two seconds and then the other in about five. Then he collapsed in a dining room chair next to Gill, his back to the grisly mess, his face a vacant stare ahead. Gill shuffled out of his seat and felt his way along the furniture and walls and then, upon finding the bathroom, he locked himself in. Calvin was slumped on the living room couch, fixedly staring at the fireplace and smoking two cigarettes, one in each hand. He was moaning over and over, "This is just awful! This is just awful!" I dashed for the kitchen, where I emptied my stomach into the trash compactor with everything I think I had ever eaten in my entire life. The cat ran and hid under the bed, her claws loosing traction as she raced across the shiny oak wood floor.

The dog was barking up a storm, and I peered out the window to see why. There was a police cruiser parked in the driveway, and two police were sitting in the car. I opened up the front door and called to Rachel to quiet down, which she did, then I called her to my side and told the police it was okay to get out of the car. Rachel came in, ran over and sniffed at the pile of towels on the floor, then crawled under the massive coffee table, her favorite spot.

The police came in, and we made nervous introductions and offered them a seat. They were suspicious as to why we sent a man in critical condition to the hospital with a fireplace poker injury to the head. At first we didn't know why the police had arrived. We hadn't thought to call them, but I suppose the call to 911 had alerted them.

It was going to be a very long night, I thought, as I eyed the crowd of neighbors milling about the street. I shut and locked the door.

We explained together. We explained separately. We explained in writing. We explained it all over again to the next group of detectives to arrive on the scene. Gill never saw a thing, his back was to Richard anyhow, and he was, of course, as blind as blind can be. The police were equally astonished to find out that not only were we engaging in a poker game, but with a blind man as well. And we had an injured neighbor, reportedly not playing poker, nearly killed by the fireplace poker. The sleeping baby in the dresser drawer was shown off repeatedly, the innocent culprit in this bizarre incident. Rita reenacted the removal of the baby from under her shirt, even waking up the baby and stuffing him under her shirt. He figured he was there to nurse and promptly seized her nipple. Rita went to pull him away and he did not want to turn loose. Finally she succeeded, but not without a mournful cry from him as she pulled him out from under her shirt for the benefit of the cops.

Soon, the house was overflowing with cops, detectives, and forensic and fingerprint specialists. Neighbors could be seen standing in the streets and their front yards, eyes trained on my house.

We reenacted the accident for the benefit of the detectives. Rita was embarrassed, and her baby was fretful at all the noise and sudden activity. I'm not even sure if poker is legal in my home state. At any rate, lots of folks are pretty religious and frown on it. Yet what a group of consenting adults do behind closed doors should be private, one would think. But it did look ominous in the newspaper stories to follow. They wrote it up like we were straight out of the Wild West, corrupting small children and killing one of our own players in the heat of a poker game.

About this time, with four cop cars out front, two more unmarked, and neighbors peeking from their windows and standing in their yards, the pizza delivery man showed up. He had a hell of a time parking. I'm sure the neighbors were impressed that in the heat of the crisis and our examination by the police, we were thoughtful enough to send out for pizza. But this was the pepperoni pizza that I had ordered just moments before Richard's accident.

The deliveryman approached the door and rang the bell. We paid him from Stephan and Calvin's change on the table as they had the most, and combined it was enough. The pizza man left the house, his eyes as big around as poker chips. The media, now camped outside, rushed at him with a flurry of questions that he couldn't answer. Shortly afterwards, a cop was stationed out front to keep the reporters at bay and to encourage people to go back home or at least stay out of the street.

We were not at all hungry, so the pizza languished on the table as the cops continued to mill about. I offered it to them and several cops grabbed a piece and munched down as other police glared at them. They were mad that the ambulance had not drawn a chalk-line around the body. They seemed to be assuming that we were a bunch of murderers. When I got up to go to the bathroom, one policeman roughly demanded to know where in the hell I thought I was going. I was startled to be so rudely treated by a stranger and in my own home. I was upset enough without the cops being nasty to me too. But they did let me go to the bathroom, and there I used the bathroom phone, the one Stephan had put in the month before, since I like to take leisurely soaks in the big old claw-footed deep oval tub. I called my business attorney, at home, and tearfully told him what was happening.

"There's been an accident, my neighbor fell down in my living room and is in critical condition, and the cops are all over us. Please come over and help us deal with this..." I whispered. He drove over to my house immediately, amazingly dressed in a very nice suit. How he got there so quickly, looking so elegant, is beyond me. I am sure he appreciated the midnight-something call that I made. He was sleeping soundly with his pregnant wife, awaiting the birth of his first child, due any day.

It was ironic that Richard hit his head with the fireplace poker while watching a poker game. Rita felt awful, but how was she to know that such a common motherly act would shock the neighbor into fainting? Even more ironic was explaining that Richard never played poker with us. He only watched. But it must have looked ominous to the police. A poker game in progress and someone gets clobbered over the head. Just an accident? Hmm, they didn't seem to think so.

What really bothered me was that if Richard had replaced the fireplace poker on its hook instead of just leaning it against the wall beside the fireplace, he wouldn't have hit his head on the thing at all. He still might have bashed his head pretty badly on the floor when he fell, but the heavy iron of the poker encountering his skull had made the injury far worse.

Then the dreaded phone call came from the hospital. Richard was officially pronounced dead. We were stunned by the horrible news. Our eccentric but dear friend was dead. We sat in a horrified and depressed silence.

And to make matters even worse, we wondered if we would all be thrown in jail. I was practically hysterical. The fire was dying as we couldn't use the poker to poke the embers, of course. The fingerprint technician was dusting the fireplace poker. As we watched the technician, we all thought about how many times we had each poked the fire during that night. Except Gill. He would warm himself in front of the fire but never poke it.

Richard had been the last to poke the fire with the poker. He had come into the house, poked the fire, and then taken up residence leaning against the doorframe. Three rounds of poker later (Stephan won one and my brother took two), Rita decided to put her baby back to bed in his dresser drawer. And then boom, Richard was down.

It stunned us all, the enormity of the situation. Even my lawyer, who was more or less hastily retained that night to represent the Thursday-Night Regulars, was a bit incredulous of the story. But that's how it happened. We had a house full of poker players, and none were witness to the accident. Money was still on the table, and a neat deck of cards lay at Stephen's seat. We had finished the last hand, and he had scraped up the deck and put it at his place, since he would deal next. Everyone swore they had seen nothing, and all avowed Richard never played. Each of us had been in a different room of the house; we all heard the accident, and none of us saw it.

Later on, looking back, I was to realize what an odd story ours must have seemed to the police. Nice house, nice neighborhood, and a nice neighbor dead in the heat of a poker game. No witnesses, but the six of us in the house, all with a common storyline that we only *heard* Richard's accident. Plus we were obviously a pretty tight clan who knew each other incredibly well.

I mean after all, it was my sister, my lover, my brother, and a very close blind friend.

After much parrying with the attorney, the police were finally convinced that we were not a threat to society and not in danger of imminent flight, so they finally relented a bit from the ominous theory of he-cheated-and-they-clobbered-him. They decided it *might* be death by misadventure and decided not to lock any of us up. Not yet.

We were relieved to have them finally leave the house around 4 a.m. We all sat down to catch our breath. The lawyer went outside and explained to the TV and newspaper crews that we were in mourning over the death of a friend and suggested that they go away. Finally a cop was assigned to guard the house to keep the harassers away the rest of the night. I was exhausted. Although Rita was spending the night with her baby, and my lover Stephen already lived there, we still had my brother and a blind player to think of getting home. It was decided they would just stay the rest of the night too and not have to venture out past the pesky media. I called my office answering machine and left a terse message that due to an extreme emergency, I would not be in that day and would explain in full on Monday.

We sat around in shocked silence munching our cold pizza and drinking herbal tea spiked with some brandy leftover from Christmas past. An evening of fun had shockingly ended with the untimely death of our friend Richard in my house.

I got up to poke the fire, only to realize that the poker had been seized for evidence. I poked it with the shovel and put some more logs on. It would be a long night of reflection. The cops had seemed angry at us, treating us like we each personally clobbered Richard. I know they were just doing their jobs, and they are trained to act that way. Yet this wasn't a crime scene, but rather a comfortable home where a very unfortunate accident had occurred. Of course we had hoped and prayed that Richard would be okay. And were shocked that he wasn't.

The next few days were filled with a blur of activity. The long awaited pathology report was released on Tuesday. The coroner determined that Richard's injury was indeed from falling backwards, possibly due to fainting, and the injury was consistent with the accident as we reported it, blah, blah, blah. We were relieved. I let the lawyer handle the unpleasant details.

The TV and newspapers had a field day. None of us wanted to be interviewed, and we certainly didn't want our names in the paper. But the police report, which reporters were permitted to read, supplied all our names, and we were dismayed to see them in print the next evening.

All day long, whenever the news played, Richard was the lead story. "Man Killed At Poker Game." The whole gruesome story was in the paper and on the news. I didn't go into work all the next week. It was too embarrassing, as I worked with about 700 clients.

Yes, that was fifteen years ago and two thousand miles away. Amazing what crafty, sensationalistic reporting can do to one's career, one's home, and one's life. My client list began dwindling as my name was now tarnished, even though I was innocent of any crime. In addition, stalwart religious clients who didn't believe in playing cards *at all* moved their accounts to another executive or left our firm all together. Things became icy between my partners and me. My earnings dwindled in a rapid, downward spiral.

Within the week, the police released my fireplace poker and closed the case. We hung flowers on Richard's door, but his family did not want to see us. We wanted to express our condolences, but they refused to speak with us. We stood on the steps in stunned silence as they shut the door in our faces. They carried Richard back to his hometown and buried him there. We were terribly saddened to say this final good-bye to our friend. We were deeply sympathetic for the suffering of his family, in spite of their coldness towards us.

That was our final poker game at Overbrook
house. Within a few months, my partners bought
me out of the firm, and I sold the house. Stephan
and I broke up, and he took the pets with him
when he moved out. After paying off the mort-
gage and the attorney, I used the leftover money
to buy a sailboat and cruise the Caribbean, picking up odd jobs here and there. I heard the pizza
parlor went broke the next year.

I forgot all about poker, never playing or
thinking about it until years later when I met
the boyz and we started playing regularly in the
Pink Papaya, first on Mondays and then later, on
Friday nights.

Slowly I brought myself back into the present
from fifteen years ago and two thousand miles
away. From a cold night at Overbrook house to
the tropical breeze I sat in now. I gazed at the
faces of the boyz, the Friday Night Regulars.
They looked stunned, and each of them stared
at me incredulously as I concluded the sad tale
of the Thursday Night Regulars and the tragedy
of Richard's death.

Riding Monkeys

Tortola attracts folks from around the world. Many speak English as a second language, and many are from Europe. One time, these two German ladies visited our island. They decided they wanted to do some horseback riding, so they went to our local riding stables. The horse owner asked them if they had ridden a horse a before. They replied in near perfect English:

"No, we have not ridden horses before, but we have ridden monkeys."

Intrigued, the horse owner asked them, "What is it like to ride a monkey?" He had never heard of such a thing but was certainly interested. Perhaps he would look into getting a few of those kinds of monkeys and offering them for rides.

"Well, you know, it was like a horse, I suppose. They put a saddle on him, and we climbed on and rode him all day. You just sort of kick him a little and off he goes, at a slow trot, no galloping."

Throughout the day, as he guided the ladies on their horseback riding adventure, he asked them more and more questions about this monkey riding. The ladies were equally puzzled that he was so keen to know about something that they thought he should already know about, but they answered all his questions.

Toward the end of the day, they said: *"Look! There is a monkey! We rode one like THAT."*

The owner craned his head around 180 degrees, only to see a donkey.

As you can imagine, all had a good laugh as he explained to the ladies the difference between a *monkey* and a *donkey*.

Sea Goddess Rose Bakes a Cake

Sick and tired of shark bites and hurricanes, I decided to make my favorite holiday recipe to cheer me up and to please the cabin boyz. They just loved it, so I will share it with you (even though usually pirates don't share at all). So, here you go, for a jump-start on your holidays, try this fruitcake recipe. I just love to make this one and hope you do, too.

You will need:

A GOOD bottle of whiskey
Assorted dried fruits
Flour
Baking powder
Salt
Eggs
Brown sugar
Butter
Vanilla flavoring
Loaf pans
And don't forget,
A GOOD bottle of whiskey

First, assemble all ingredients. Carefully measure out a cup of whiskey and test for quality.

Use electric mixer to cream the butter with the sugar.

Pour a cup and a half of whiskey and sample for purity.

In separate bowl, combine flour, pacing bowder and salt.

Sample tree tablespoons of whiskey for authenticity.

Break a legg into bowl.

Thip wourghly.

Heat up oven.

About three fifty to four, (close one eye for better adjustment of temperature.)

Check whiskey for freshness.

Mix blour, futter, sugar and leggs all together.

Add a flop of vanilla dravoring.

Toss in fried druid.

(Hiccup) I mean, floss in fruit flies.

Pour into loaf hand by pan.

Check whiskey for alkeyhol content.

Bake for sexy minutes.

Finish whiskey, before bottle goes bad.

Check for doneness by inserting tooth prick.

(Hiccup) I mean pooth tick.

If it rings spack, it is done.

Spit on cooling rack, till okay to fwap with fwoil.

Pry a titty ribbon around fwoil into a bow.
Deliver to your amazed fiends and fellatives.
   A relicious decipe. (Hiccup!) Bone-Tap-A-Feat!

From the kitchen of ZeaRoze
(hiccup!)

Three At Sea

From Grace Klutz
Aboard the Frying Crowd
In a secluded anchorage
18 in the latitudes
With changes in attitudes

Dear Mom,

It was a very hot day in the Caribbean. I was sailing aboard Don's boat. We had purposely chosen an anchorage off a secluded beach for a few days, hoping to get a bit of boat work done. Things are always breaking and falling apart, that never-ending nightmare we call boat ownership.

You know what *boat* really stands for, Mom? It *really* means *Break Out Another Thousand.*

Well, anyway, we could enjoy running around the boat naked, a freedom from tan lines and the restraint and bindings of clothes. Not to mention what we save on our laundry bill, as well as on general wear and tear. The sun tends to bake the very life out of clothes. I know, because all my clothes of the past have eventually been shredded for the ragbag, polishing and cleaning bits of my boat over the years.

Being from the modest Southern states of the U.S.A., I wouldn't have dared dream I would find myself running around naked in the Caribbean one day. Yet, Mom, I think almost all Southerners that ever roamed the numerous lakes and rivers dotting the mountains must have had at least *one* skinny-dipping event under their bellybutton.

I remember when I was a young teenager, very young (so young you might not approve of what we were doing); I was on a double date. Remember Leonard? He was five years older than me, and he was only eighteen. My brother (fifteen) was on a date with a girl we always referred to as The Preacher's Daughter. I remember you were proud, Mom, to have your son dating The Preacher's Daughter.

One evening, Leonard showed up in his shiny red Chevy Nova. He had The Preacher's Daughter with him. Still I can picture the look on your face when Nathaniel casually told you that he and I were going to the movies with Leonard and The Preacher's Daughter. You were shocked, but you knew Leonard, and he did come from Shady Elms, the upscale neighborhood that fringed our middle-class suburb. We thought you'd never let me go out on a date, so that's why Nathaniel and Leonard worked it out to invite The Preacher's Daughter, too. I'm so glad you let me go. We had a grand time making-out at the drive-in movies, then afterwards we smoked a doobie, then picked up a pizza and ate it in the car cause we liked the stereo system. It was this really cool eight-track and Leonard had loads of tapes. We took The Preacher's Daughter home, and I came home, safe, sound and on time, much to your relief.

Nearly every night I went out with Leonard, but we didn't always go to the movies. Sometimes we drove up to the mountains and just rode around, listening to music, and smoking a joint.

As the saying goes, it was a hot summer's night. Our usual foursome had been riding around the mountains. We stopped near our old summer cabin up at the river. We hiked down to the river's edge in the glorious moonlit night. Earlier we had been stargazing at Bald Rock.

Leonard, Nathaniel, The Preacher's Daughter and I stood by the river's edge surrounded by beautiful evergreens. The water was mesmerizing, gurgling as it meandered around the river rocks and over the felled-tree dam. Yes, of course, you know the spot, where that old man used to stack up rock sculptures. I remember there were probably five or six and another few in progress. He was married to that crazy artist I spent the summer with one year.

I forget the discussion, it probably lasted all of ninety seconds before we were all naked and in the river, freezing. We were trying to swim around to stay warm, but not wanting to bump into each other. It was *cold* but so refreshing. I remember on the long drive home, we kept the windows rolled down in the summer's heat, not using the air-conditioning. The Preacher's Daughter and I needed to dry out our long hair. (It's a shame I'm not there to see the shock on your face, Mama!)

So now, twenty-something years later, we're anchoring a boat in the Caribbean (in the National Park waters, as we soon find out). But it's not the usual foursome. Leonard now has five kids with what's-her-face, Nathaniel works in some God-forsaken factory, and I heard The Preacher's Daughter was caught in a scandal with a married woman at a gay club.

Now, it is just Don and I. The secluded beach off to our starboard side can only be reached by donkey trail or dinghy. The people on the beach are mostly nude or wearing itsy-bitsy tongs to cover up their t'ings.

Lil Steve was ashore at the beach. He saw us and waved, then jumped in the water and swam out to our boat. He climbed on board in his birthday suit, we still in ours. I owed him $50 for previous services performed. Lest this sound ominous, I could tell you it was for his professional masseuse services in taking care of my injured shoulder, or I could tell you it was for a bag of pot. Actually, at this point and time, I no longer remember why I owed him the $50, but I paid him that day. When I paid him, he giggled that he had no pockets. So he folded the bill into fourths and held it in his left hand.

And, as the saying goes, it was a hot summer's day, and we all decided a swim in the sea would be good thing. The shady palm trees ashore were beckoning me for an afternoon nap after a cooling swim. But due to my shoulder injury, there was no way I could swim all the way to the beach from the boat. Don and Lil Steve are both quite muscular, and it would have been no problem for them, but since I was taking the dinghy in, they rode with me.

In our glee, we didn't bother with clothes or towels. It was so hot that the sun would bake us dry after swimming. We didn't have that far to go, maybe three hundred yards. Just the three of us naked, and the fifty-dollar bill. The people on the nude beach were watching our approach. We were driving a two-horse engine, which is about the speed of a brisk rowboat.

Out of nowhere, a Park Ranger came speeding up to us in a huge Boston Whaler. Our two-horse could only go so fast and before we could get to the beach, this park ranger was on top of us looking down in the dinghy. Don whispered,

"Act natural." Now what an oxymoron that is. "Act natural". Here we are in our birthday suits on a pleasant Sunday afternoon.

We thought he was stopping us for being naked, but he was stopping us for not using the new unmarked channel entrance. Or, so he said.

He stared at us. There were two oars laying on the floorboards, but no clothes or towels. He stares at Lil Steve who had his left hand in a tight fist. He asked him what's he holding and to open up his hand.

Very slowly, so as not to have the money blow away, Lil Steve opened up his fist to reveal the folded up fifty-dollar bill. The Officer sized up the money and the three of us. He asked us what we are up to.

I looked at the now empty beach; at least it was empty of people, but not their possessions. You see, folks at the beach get undressed and hang their clothes, backpacks, hats, glasses, small coolers, towels, sarongs, bathing suits, scarves, and what-have-you on the sea grape trees. This keeps everything dry and out of the sand.

Today, with the beachgoers cowering in the woods, the beach resembled an exotic bazaar with various merchandise exotically displayed. Given the beachgoers' propensity for tie-dyed fabrics as well as batik, it was quite a colorful scene and I wished I'd had a camera. I know,

Mom, I should have been wishing for clothes or a towel, but I was wishing for a camera, as it would have made a great shot.

The nude sunbathers were hiding in the woods behind the beach because of the Park Ranger. He looked at us, and he looked at the beach. A few moments before, it had been teeming with nudists; now only a few folks were in the water, conveniently up to their necks, pretending not to notice the Park Ranger and us. They hadn't time to exit the water and run for cover, so they just stayed up to their necks in water.

No one answered, so the Park Ranger repeated himself. I think it's pretty obvious that we are headed for the beach, which everyone knows is mostly nude. Instead, Lil Steve told him we are going ashore to buy some clothes. He looked at us long and hard, taking in our sun tanned bodies and our lack of modesty (how much can you hide behind an oar?). Looking longingly at the beach, wishing I was there instead of here listening to this officer, I spied the funniest sight. Judy was on the beach, and she was pregnant with her second child. He was due any moment and she spent the hot days laying at the beach under a palm tree in a hammock her husband tied up for her.

Judy was sleeping and the rush of people heading for the cover of the woods woke her up in her hammock. Seeing the Park Ranger she had rolled out of the hammock and was trying unsuccessfully to hide behind the palm tree. But I could see that huge belly poking out, and it made the tree look sort of deformed, as the tan of her skin was about the same color as the tree.

The Park Ranger realized no further explanation was forthcoming. In my mind, I was thinking, well, we are naked, we have money, and we are shopping for clothes. Some story, Mom.

I guess the Park Ranger decided to buy our story and accept our apologies for not using the unmarked channel. Now that we knew where the unmarked channel was, we would surely use it next time, and so… we went shopping for clothes. He sped away from us as fast as he came. We continued on ashore as the nudists began emerging from the woods laughing at us.

Someone asked what the ranger wanted. We replied he wanted us to be aware of the unmarked channel for beach entrance by dinghy.

"Weren't you all embarrassed?"

"No, we just acted *naturally*."

Love and hugs,
Grace

The Unwreck of Rose Royce

I have been busy trying to be ingenious; what a chore! But the end result is, I now have a real desk for my office-cum-home. Built it myself from a $22 tinker toy set (used). My downstairs neighbors were moving out and I (like others would do too) eyed the whole place like a cat sniffing it out, looking to see if there is anything they had that I want and they might sell, since they are moving back to their charter boat (as Elf-employed crew; rampant rum-rumors are that the elves chartered them for Santa's Caribbean Christmas Visit).

Anyhow, I see they have these two tall shelves built out of tinker toys. They are bragging that they found them used at a used store in St Thomas. (Guess they don't do dumpster shopping like me!) These apartments we rent come semi-furnished eclectically, although I like my collection okay. There are no used shops on Tortola that I know of. I think stuff is so hard to get and falls apart before it could be resold, although I find some very useful stuff in the dumpsters I frequent. (I could pass the civil service exam here and correctly list off all the dumpster locations on the island. This is in part from hauling garbage when I work as a private chef, in various exotic vacation villas around the islands.)

Anyhow, I bought the tinker toy shelves from them even though I didn't need shelves, but the fact that they looked useful struck a chord in the back of my nutty head. They wanted $24 for them. I dumped out my purse and could only find $22 and two cents. They even carried them upstairs for me. I was dashing off to check on my mechanic and deliver his mumbo-jumbo-bucket to the boat plus give him a ride home (yeah, his jeep really is totaled, really awful; you'd have thought somebody died in it, it looks so bad). Of course he is the butt of some ribbing, such as, "How'd you total your jeep without even getting out of the parking lot?"

He wanted an advance on the boat engine work, and I said "No, I will advance you money for parts, and the minute it purrs again, I will pay you in cash every penny you ask for. Then you'll have a big lump-sum to buy yourself a very-used-vehicle, and I will be a happy broke-again sailor!" In the meantime, I tried to give him rides, and since he is popular, he doesn't have any trouble if I don't show.

I am mortified that Pits 'N' Power-Piss (a ficti-tious name changed for obvious reasons) charged me $1200 and pronounced the boat engine running fine, and it ran for only ten minutes. I am trying to get the bank to reverse the charge card without much luck! Twice mortified!

The new/used mechanic is not from Pits 'N' Power-Piss, but he is doing this work for me in his spare time (he is overworked with his own fleet) because he feels awful that he wasn't the one to fix it for me to begin with. I understand lawsuits here are practically impossible, and I am furious that Pits & Power-Piss can so ruthlessly rob people.

Back to the tinker toys; I studied the two tall shelving units when I got home later and decided I could disassemble and reassemble them into an L-shaped desk for my computer and peripheral office paraphernalia.

Man, what a comedy! I felt like I was trapped in one of those hilarious cartoons where no matter what you do, the elements beat human. No sooner would I pop a widget from a corner, three sides would pop out and flail at me. I'd pop it back together the way I wanted it and then discover I was three thumbs short of popping in another crucial piece. At one point, the thing exploded in pieces as I removed a widget and parts went flying out onto the balcony. One of the widgets escaped to the ground below, and I never found it.

It became a real slapstick, how-not-to-do-it comedy as I battled with these flat panels and these ingenious widgets that are supposed to connect the panels together. I'd make a lousy engineer, I guess. I kept having to disassemble and reassemble, cause if you don't get the widget placed just right, then two panels later, you are screwed.

Finally I got the L shaped desk built. But then I decided that it would look better as one long sleek desk rather than L-shaped. A few more hours later and (whew!) I finally had my sleek long desk built, and my vocabulary had increased with frightening words, I shall not repeat.

I scooted up to the new desk in my came-with-the-apartment plastic chair (the cheap kind sold for outdoor use; bucket seat with arms) and discovered it was slung lower than the table and typing would be very uncomfortable. What I needed was a standard chair—or a real luxury, an office chair. Neither was in my budget. I mean, I'm the little lady trying to assemble a $500 desk out of $22 in used parts. I figured I'd just have to settle for sitting on the San Juan phonebook the apartment came with, courtesy of the former Puerto Rican tenant. Now I really felt like a child with my tinker-toy desk, sitting on a phonebook to type.

Fortunately, Lady Luck intervened, and Bomba received a 2-page fax on my fax machine, which meant I had to hop in the jeep and go deliver it to him. I went to his shack and found a small party was in force. I hung out for a while, staring longingly out to sea, watching the waves break over the reef and rocks on his part of the surf-me north shore.

It began to get dark, and I rarely stay out after dark unless I have to work, so I headed back home. As I turned to go up Zion Hill Road, I scanned the roadside dumpster wishing there was a chair there for me. I slammed on the brakes, thinking Bomba must have secretly fed me some of his world famous magic mushrooms! I was hallucinating for sure! There sat a tangle of chairs in the dirt beside the dump. I stared at them and they refused to vanish, so I yanked up on my hand brake and gingerly stepped out of the jeep to see if what I saw was a dream or not. I touched the chairs, and they felt real!

Five chairs, all in good shape. I took the best two, as it was all I could fit in my tiny jeep, what with all the other junk living in there (catering cooler, spare tire, tool box, water jugs, Harpo's blanket, a bag of dented canned goods I bought at half-price, shoes, a box of spare jeep and boat parts, chains, ropes, whips *just kidding!*, plus the fender that fell off my jeep last week, *no kidding!*). Even so, one chair stuck out at an odd angle, and I prayed it would make it over the treacherous climb to the top of Zion Hill.

I can't zip the vinyl roof down the back of the jeep, cause all the zipper seams blew out in

Hurricane Marilyn of '95 or '96. I was on one island and the jeep on another, tightly zipped up. Those hurricane winds just ripped them all apart. So now the rear window portion is rolled up and snapped to the roof. It has been that way for so long in the Caribbean sun that it refuses to uncurl, even if it did have functional zippers.

At home, I hefted the chairs up to my apartment, marveling that I made it over Zion Hill without losing them. I discovered that one of them worked excellently as my desk chair. I was ready to move all my computer stuff off the kitchen bar counter, which had served as my desk since I moved in. But boy, am I ever glad I didn't rush into t'ings. After spending a whole day trying to build a desk out of tinker-toys, I was exhausted, so I went to bed without moving anything.

The next morning I woke up thinking I'd had the silliest dream of finding chairs at the dumpster. I stumbled into the kitchen to make the first of many cups of coffee and tripped right over my new/used chairs! I had to touch them to make sure they were real and I was really awake.

Unfortunately, before I could set up shop, someone yelled from outside, "Upstairs! Upstairs!" so I went on the balcony carrying my coffee cup, and d'is mon be telling me I gots to clean off the balcony, cause they are going to paint the outside of the building. I stare up at the big chunks of peeling paint along the columns and ceiling of the balcony and said, "Really? Wow, what a nice Christmas this is going to be!" He said they were going to power wash it first. (Sounded impressive and easier than scraping, but not as effective, it turned out.)

Of course I had placed my newfangled desk under the windows, and the windows don't shut tightly, so I altered my day's plans, even though there were places I needed to be. I decided to stay at home cause I didn't know these guys, and I've seen how some folks can work really sloppy around here.

I cleaned everything off the balcony, which was my dining room, den, and front yard, so it took awhile. As soon as I finished, these guys took a break and vanished. *Poof!* They had watched me laboriously remove the strings of lights wrapped around the railings. One string came with the apartment; here it is okay to keep your Christmas lights up year round and use them for ambient outdoor lighting. Mine are all white anyhow. I had augmented the original set with a newer set bought the day I was looking for a cheap kitchen faucet. Mine had exploded and hit the ceiling when the water came back on after Hurricane Lenny. Then a few days later, the power zapped on and off a few times and fried one of the white Christmas light (ahem) balcony light strings.

Mon, d'is island life be something different!

Anyhow, d'ese would-be power-washers and painters be gone, mon, so I dash over to the secret machine shop because I forgot to go there Friday and the job I have for the recluse reposing there is sort of urgent (involving the dead diesel in my boat). Plus I noticed that the time was after his Saturday morning cartoons were over. It's best not to disturb him about work until they are; I've known him long enough to know that by now. I reached there but was very embarrassed because I meant to stop at the store first and pick up the requisite bottle of wine or liquor to scribble the work order on (this speeds up service considerably).

After I explained to him what I think the new/ used mechanic wants done to this part, I apologized profusely for not going to the store first (but promised to dash right out and return). As I spoke, I looked across the harbor and saw that my apartment building appeared to be on fire— smoke was billowing wildly out of it! My heart skipped quite a few beats, like being suspended in time; you know you are here, but your heart isn't sure yet.

Geez! This was the second time this week that my heart had gone a-flutter with dread, the first being the day I thought I had died in a massive freak auto accident. See, the other day I was racing along the waterfront in my jeep. As I approached this flat curve on the water's edge, a big gust of wind hit me. I chastised myself for driving fast. I was uncharacteristically in a hurry, and I knew that this curve was often met with strong gusts of wind from the ocean.

First the jeep seemed to shutter from the onslaught, then there was a big bang. The jeep was hit by a massive jolt, a vibrant flash of red engulfed my entire vision, and then I was blinded! I mean, I think when folks are killed in car wrecks, there is a big bang, a jolt, lots of red blood, and then you can't see anymore because you are dead. So, here I thought I was dead!

It appeared I was traveling at 90 miles an hour, but in reality I was probably at my top limit, a whopping 40 miles an hour (the speedometer/odometer died two summers ago). I'm not sure how, but even though I was blind and dead, I somehow had presence of mind to remember the shape of the curve in minute detail and guided the jeep accordingly. I slowed to a stop while turning the car slightly to follow around the curve, even though I could not see the road at all. All I could see was a wall of red.

I was afraid to slam on the brakes because that is what makes these little jeeps flip over sometimes. (I know, I saw that once too and was ever so grateful I wasn't a driver or a passenger, but I did stop to help rescue, a whole n'other story from years ago.)

Anyhow, as my jeep slowed to a complete stop, I realized I might be ALIVE because I was uncontrollably shaking from head to toe like a palm frond in a hurricane. I then noticed that my windshield-mounted rearview mirror had been fixed by the wreck! It had been stuck in the same place for years, making me have to crane my neck to see out of it; but there it was, swiveled into a new position. I sat there playing with the mirror until I got it the way I wanted it and even peeked into it to reaffirm the fact that I was not dead after all.

That's when I noticed the hood against the windshield. The windshield hadn't a crack in it at all, but the hood was resting firmly against it. Finally it began to dawn upon me what had happened. The red hood of the jeep had flown open and squarely hit the windshield. The shocking jar must have been me hitting another car, and the big bang was the jeep hood hitting the windshield. Dim reality crept further into my dazed brain. Nothing appeared to bleeding about me at all! Wow!

Since I was alive, I gingerly limped and crawled out of my jeep to go see how the other guy faired. I wondered if he was dead or just thought he was. I said a silent prayer that there wouldn't be a whole bunch of dead people in a mangled car. I even remember taking a deep breath to brace myself for the carnage that I was sure to encounter. I had not looked at the rest of my jeep at all; I just didn't want to know. I was moving around on autopilot, thinking of the international law of the sea of rescuing injured folks first. I had no idea what the hell had happened.

But as I surveyed the scene, I saw no other wreck. So I hobbled across the road to go peer in the ocean; perhaps the other vehicle was knocked in the sea?

Last spring I came upon a recent one-car wreck and the sole vehicle was sitting in the ocean with all four sides mashed in, the roof caved in, and all the windows shattered. The new owner was on his first spin in his brand new car. He drove along the waterfront at full speed with the super-tinted windows up to savor the stereo at maximum volume and to delight in the comfort of full-blast air-conditioning. He was fiddling around with the tape player when he hit one of our numerous infamous potholes, the car became airborne and sailed right over the low sea wall, splashed in the ocean at a depth too low to be diving, and rolled a 360, landing on all fours again.

So, I scrunched up my good eye and scanned the sea. I didn't see a car or body or anything. I must be dead after all and HEAVEN has an ocean!

I slowly turned back to see if my jeep was still there. It was. The front was still intact, and there were no new dents. I wobbled across the road to find out what the hell happened.

By now, I wondered again if I were alive or dead or dreaming. I mean one big wreck and there's no blood and no damage to the jeep, and the other car has vanished.

Ah, I saw that the hood latch had parted company again, and the safety chain, which is a bicycle lock-chain, had exploded right at the latch. Normally the hood shouldn't been have able to lift more than five or six inches, even with the hood latch broken.

So apparently I had hit a huge pothole, the hood latch had popped off, the bicycle chain had exploded at the hood latch, thus allowing the red jeep hood to fly up and hit the windshield. The shock of all of this had put me into a daze, but now it was all coming together. Life was making sense again, and I was thrilled that everything was more or less okay.

I suppose you are wondering why I keep my hood locked with a bicycle chain. That is because the dear Rose Royce (yes, my ancient red jeep) is probably the most disreputable looking piece of machinery to continue plying these roads. It used to be that whenever I parked my jeep, opportunists would mistake it for a broken-down wreck and swipe parts off of it. This is what is locally known as "shopping for used jeep parts" since buying them new and paying the 20 or 25 percent duty on top of shipping and dealer markups makes them hideously expensive and hard to obtain. So not much inventory is kept on the island. I lost a whole carburetor once before I got that lock! It was hell getting another carburetor, and I was in the middle of a Private Chef assignment on the top of nowhere at a villa you'd never find if you hadn't been first escorted there personally. I had to pirate another jeep just to finish the week out!

Anyhow, since then, I put a bicycle chain-lock on my hood to let the opportunists know that these are MY parts, so precious that I lock them up. Funny thing is, I've been stopped by strangers who are dying to know what is under my hood! One guy came up to me in the Wrong-way Supermarket parking lot a few weeks ago as I was loading my jeep.

"You want to sell me d'at jeep?" he asks.

"No, I want to drive it!" I tell him.

"D'at jeep so ugly! Whacha hiding under d'at hood? Must be a reason you keep driving it. You got some sort of special engine in there? I seen d'is jeep all over the place, mon. D'at hood always be locked up."

"Yes," I tell him, "This is the seventh island it has been on." I noticed him eyeing all the duct-tape on the jeep, so I added, "And yes, I happen to like duct-tape."

At the time, the fender, before it fell off completely later in the week, was bandaged up with copious amounts of duct-tape, as was part of the body covering the engine. A rust hole had formed there allowing rain to fall on my electrical wires, which shorted out half of everything. But duct-tape fixes all, at least temporarily, so I like it.

He squeaked his teeth loudly and laughed out loud. "No shit! You like d'at duct tape! Cheese and bread, mon!" he said with more teeth squeaking, and a firm shaking of his head, and we both laughed like crazy as I backed out of my parking spot.

When I finally got back home, I found that the apartment wasn't on fire after all. They were just power washing with great glee, and from afar the mist had appeared to be smoke. Sure enough, quite a bit had managed to spray inside; but what the heck, I had been meaning to mop anyhow. Next they painted the balcony, barely managing to get more on the walls and roof than on the floor. So now I got to buy a scraper to tidy up the dropped blobs they missed and clean up the paint they tracked throughout the place.

Nevertheless, it was a splendid week in paradise! I've got a great desk and a chair for my home office, my boat engine is in a million parts with promises it soon will be reassembled, my apartment didn't burn down, and my balcony is repainted. And of course, to top it all off, I didn't die in a terrible vehicle accident after all. I survived to write about the unwreck of Rose Royce.

Thank God for miracles! I'd hate to have a life without them!

Shanghai

Delilah landed at the St Thomas airport, her charter was over in Puerto Rico and fresh money lined her pocket. She walked the half-mile from the airport to the bus stop where she waited for another forty-odd minutes. When the bus pulled up, she boarded wearily, sweat dripping down her forehead. She welcomed the cool air conditioning and looked forward to sitting down on a soft seat. Delilah would be the only white person on the bus, but she didn't care; she was accustomed to traveling in foreign places. While she fumbled for the correct change (the buses refused to make change), she was rudely told by the bus driver that luggage was not allowed on the bus. Well, what was she to do with her backpack and carry-on? They certainly weren't very big.

Delilah looked down the length of the bus, crowded with West Indians, grocery bags, bags from Woolworth, and huge plastic and cloth shopping bags with nice carrying handles. She stared at the bus driver, but he yelled at her to get off the bus and go take a taxi. She despised losing her chance at the cheap fare. It was so unfair, she thought as she disembarked the bus. It had now been over an hour-and-a-half since she had landed. The old-fashioned luggage system had taken over forty-five minutes to spit out the few bags from the small flight.

The only cool place in the airport was the lounge. So Delilah could either start walking in the sweltering heat or sit and rest a few moments in the cool bar with a pricey drink. Delilah had a rum punch while she considered her next options.

After finishing her drink, she slowly walked back across the street, through the parking lot, and across the drop-off lanes where taxis had the best parking. She wearily approached the dispatcher, who ignored her as he shouted instructions at other passengers and drivers. The taxi dispatcher at the airport was the rudest of all the people on the island. Adding insult to injury, non-couple passengers had to pay a surcharge to ride in the taxi vans, even though they would be forced to endure numerous stops.

After a few minutes, he glared at her and barked, "Where to?"

"Yacht Heaven Marina, please."

"Stand here!"

He waved his arms about, shouting in passengers' faces, "Where to?" and then shoving them off toward various taxis. Delilah stood in the heat, first on one foot, then the other.

She picked up her bags and headed for the restroom. She wanted to splash some water in her parched mouth, there being no water fountains at the airport. She came back out of the restroom and headed for the dispatcher.

"Come!" yelled the dispatcher to a startled Delilah. "Get in that taxi! Yacht Heaven?"

He practically shoved Delilah towards a van parked several spaces away. It was already piled high with tourist luggage, and people were squeezed like sardines in the back seats. Lucky for Delilah, since she was alone she got to ride in the front seat with her bags piled on her feet. With a banging of doors, the driver hopped in and took off at breakneck speed and then slammed on breaks momentarily to say "hi" to the parking lot attendant. Then he floored the accelerator as they careened out of the parking lot and down a road covered with potholes. He raced around the irregular ruts, often in the wrong lane, sometimes narrowly missing oncoming traffic. The passengers were silent as they stared out the tinted windows. Suddenly the taxi made a swerve to the right, with two cars barreling down on him. Barely missing them, he turned into a hotel parking lot and slammed on breaks at the lobby entrance.

Two passengers in the rear spoke up; it was their stop. Someone opened the sliding door. The entire van emptied out to let the couple off.

The driver hopped out, ran around to the back of the van, threw open the doors, and asked the couple to point out their bags. He grabbed their bags and rearranged a few of the others, stashing them at impossible angles. He demanded his fare and was paid by the couple with a twenty. It took him an eternity it seemed, to dive into his pockets and slowly, ever so slowly, count out the change to the tourists.

He carefully rubbed each one-dollar bill, making a production of counting it out, and rubbing the next bill just as meticulously, as if each one had to be smoothed over before he reluctantly turned loose of it. The tourists gave up, leaving him a hefty tip. He did not offer to carry their luggage to the desk, nor was there a bellhop to assist.

He jumped in the van, sped out of the hotel, and pulled out in front of a small Honda. He tooted his horn, muttering something unintelligible to the Honda.

After a mile, they made a sudden left turn, heading up into the hills. Delilah groaned; she'd been on the taxi for a half-hour now, for what should have been a twenty-minute trip. She slumped in her seat, wondering if she would make it to the marina before sunset.

To complicate the taxi system, taxis are only allowed to discharge at hotels, but not allowed to pick up there unless it is their regular stand.

Makes no sense at all, but leaves lots of empty taxi vans roaming around the island. Indeed, if you drop off passengers at the airport, it would make sense to get in line and pick up a new fare, but no, the taxis must leave the airport empty and return to their usual hang outs. Strange indeed, but this way, you have worse traffic jams in St Thomas. Too many taxis and most of them empty, trying to fight traffic back to their pick-up stations.

Delilah endured another hour on the taxi, making numerous hotel stops. She was tired and weary. She still had to find a place to stay or a crew position. The traffic to Yacht Heaven slowed to a crawl. Not only was it now rush hour, but also the streets were clogged with vans returning passengers to the cruise ship docks. Oncoming traffic was clogged with empty taxi vans, delivery trucks, and lone drivers in private cars along with a smattering of rental jeeps with nervous tourists learning to drive on the left side of the road.

The driver crept forward toward the hotel entrance to Yacht Heaven. Delilah pointed out she wanted the marina entrance, a block ahead and two over on the right. He could deposit her at the usual drop-off circle, on the other side of the marina parking lot.

The driver told her to get out. Right there, while they were clogged in traffic. Delilah was tired, and she knew the walk to the marina would be longer from here as she carried her bags. She'd waited half the day to fly on stand-by, waited an hour for luggage, and ditto for the bus that refused her. An hour more and she was *finally* near her destination, but this taxi driver did not want to take her the final few blocks. She had just spent two weeks on board a luxury yacht as crew. She treated her customers as number one.

All the tourist couples had been dumped at the hotel lobby of their choice. She had endured seven stops, most out of the way. Now she was being put out in oncoming traffic, in the middle of the street.

He barked a fare at her. She knew it was triple the normal. She was being charged for traveling *alone* as well as extra for each bag that sat on her feet. The bus she had tried to board had reached the marina over an hour-and-a-half ago for only a dollar.

She made a split decision. Today, Delilah discovered she had a bit of piracy in her after all. Delilah, who had always paid her way, worked hard, helped others even to the point of being taken advantage of, decided that enough was enough. She lived out of her bags, worked on various sailboats, yachts, ships and deliveries. She accumulated nothing and therefore had nothing for others to take away. "Freedom's just another word for nothing left to lose," as the song says.

So she grabbed her bags and stepped out of the air-conditioned taxi. The driver looked at her expectantly, holding out his greedy palm. She slammed the door and darted through the oncoming traffic to the opposite sidewalk. She began heading for the hotel lobby, which opened into a garden and eventually led to the marina entrance. Behind her, the taxi van honked furiously. While quickening her pace, she looked over her shoulder to see if he was going to be able to thread through the traffic snarl to reach her.

The taxi driver leaned over the seat, rapidly rolled down the passenger window, and yelled across traffic for her to come pay. Cars behind him began honking as traffic tired of waiting on him. She saw that he could not possibly turn into the hotel, so she yelled back, "You should have taken me where I asked you to. I'd have paid you full fare, and a big tip too!" With that said, she triumphantly strode through the lobby and out the side entrance into the lush tropical garden. She trotted to the restrooms by the pool.

Inside the ladies room she took a shower of sorts from the sink basin. A hand written sign, resembling a first grade project, admonished her not to bathe her *feets* in the sink. She did so anyhow. Using an immense amount of paper towels, she washed herself from head to toe, then dried off. Combing out her long hair she twisted and braided it expertly into a French braid. She changed into a purple tank top, tied a colorful sarong at her waist, and spritzed herself with some of her favorite perfume *Obsession*.

She came out of the restroom quite refreshed. Strolling over to the pool, she took a stool at the bar and ordered ginger ale. She saw the taxi driver arrive at the marina entrance and slam on brakes. He got out and looked all around him. His eyes danced right past her at the garden bar. He did not recognize her, nor did he see her bags stashed under her stool. He walked down to the docks, only to return a few minutes later. Delilah figured he was checking the other bar and the outdoor bistro for signs of his non-paying fare.

Delilah finished the last of her ginger ale. The driver reappeared, got in his van, and drove off in a tire-screeching huff. Delilah, the new-found pirate, giggled to herself. Perhaps she would have never done such an outrageous act had she not been so tired and weary.

Ah, the transportation in St Thomas, something that could easily be improved but never would be. She tipped the bartender, and then ambled through the luscious garden, enjoying the exotic beauty. Eventually, she exited through the iron gates to the mall and marina entrance. She would start with the largest dock and the biggest yachts, inquiring about crew positions. First she stopped at the outdoor bulletin board. She read the notices.

6 hp outboard for sale, needs work...

Charter cook needed...(for two months ago)

Bunks for rent on the Taj Mahal, $15/nite...

Female crew wanted to go down island with young 70 year old...

To Captain Mo, I come, you go, I see no Mo, Now I gone, not here no mo', sea you in Margaritaville next month, CC.

For Sale, everything must go, leaving island...

REWARD for return of Rover, big black Labrador, real friendly, loves swimming and boats, last seen Sunday at Water Island Beach Party. Return to s/v Footloose...

Bartender, Cook, Wait staff wanted. Apply in person at The Virgin Oar House

Hurricane mooring for sale...

Couple wanted for delivery to the Med...

Delilah had just finished reading the board when a tall, young man sauntered over purposely. He had long black wavy hair gathered into a loose ponytail. His t-shirt was faded, with a slight tear on the back shoulder. The white material contrasted nicely with his deep tan. His shorts appeared to have put in some heavy-duty time, but were still in tact. His tanned feet were jammed into an antique pair of leather Docksiders with knotted tassels battling with each other. His sunglasses were attached to a colorful cord around his neck.

Somewhere in the depths of the ocean, there are fish wearing designer sunglasses, many of them prescription, for lack of a simple cord.

His angular face appeared to have been shaved sometime in the past week or perhaps he just had a ferocious mid-morning shadow. Definitely, a professional sailor. That quintessential look. The subtle identifying traits that enables one seafarer to pick out another.

He stared at the bulletin board. Delilah approached. She cleared her throat and turned towards the man.

"Are you looking for work?" Well, at least it's a conversation starter, thought Delilah.

"No. I am looking for crew."

How convenient, she thought as her heart skipped a beat.

"To do what?"

"To help me deliver a sloop to Annapolis." *(Funny, I been there before)*

"Oh. When are you leaving?" *(I'm already packed.)*

"Soon as I find one or two crew." *(Interesting...)*

"Oh. Well. Hmm... I might be interested. *(Sell me.)*

He looked her over, appraising her seaworthiness. Then he stuck his hand out and said, "Hi, my name is Johan." He pronounced it *Yohan*. "But just call me Arnie."

"My name is Delilah."

She felt his nice warm hand and noted some calluses, typical of many sailors.

They began talking and wandered over to the umbrella bistro tables outside the deli. A few people were having cold drinks and sandwiches. The place was legendary and was where many sailors hung out, swapping lies and trading sea tales.

Verbally, Arnie and Delilah exchanged their respective curriculum vitae. Delilah prayed he wasn't another drunken ill-mannered captain, as she tried to size him up. He was quite nice looking, and he wasn't flirting with her. Some captains only hire women who will share their bunk. Arnie assured Delilah that the sailboat had plenty of bunks. He seemed nice enough, with an impressive background, if he could be believed. He thought her modest sailing credentials sufficient enough to make the trip with him.

Delilah agreed to go for the slight pay offered, plus return airfare, payable up-front. She stipulated a third crewmember. The boat did not have auto-helm. Delilah figured it would be far too taxing for only two people to make such an arduous journey without a third person to help steer. He agreed.

That evening, Delilah moved aboard the boat, which was tied up stern-to at a concrete wharf. The vessel was a 38-foot sloop named *Shanghai*. Still being quite the novice, Delilah did not realize what sad shape the boat was really in. Arnie, on the other hand did know, but he did not care. He was being paid a handsome rate as delivery captain. That was all he cared about.

Over drinks at The-Hole-In-Wall-Bar, Delilah discovered Arnie was from Switzerland. They had fun exchanging notes on American life versus Swiss versus the Caribbean lifestyle. He wanted to leave the next day, but Delilah reminded him they still needed that third crewmember. Arnie tried to tell her just the two of them could make it. She refused to consider the idea.

Only seven people sat in the bar. None were interested in the trip. No one knew of anyone who was. Arnie and Delilah left and walked to the Reef Bar, another of the local watering holes where sailors hung out. They ordered drinks and inquired around for crew. Ironically, they were having a hard time finding anyone interested in going. Usually there was no shortage of crew looking to return to the mainland. But it was late in the season, so perhaps many had already departed. The third member would not be paid in cash. Only room, board, and airfare back.

They ordered Caesar Salads with teriyaki steak, and then returned to *Shanghai* to sleep until sunrise.

In the morning Arnie busied himself checking the boat and sent her by gypsy cab to the airport. There Delilah retrieved a life raft that looked like it had flown around the world, it had so many airline tags affixed to it. On the way back to the marina, Delilah had the taxi drop her at the grocery store. She asked him to wait, since the life raft was in the back of his station wagon. She hurried through the store, amassing fresh fruits and vegetables, along with some canned soups and sandwich makings. She bought ginger ale and crackers by the case, her offshore food for preventing seasickness. The boat had no refrigeration, so she bought four blocks of ice.

She tipped the bag boy, who helped her lug everything to the taxi. To her relief, the gypsy was waiting for her, still parked illegally. In St Thomas taxis have a penchant for parking anywhere and everywhere for as long as they care. Stopping in the middle of the street to discharge passengers into oncoming traffic was permissible too. In the Virgin Islands, everyone drives on the left side of the road, but incongruously, the cars all have left-side steering wheels. The taxi vans only have sliding doors on the right side of the vehicle. It all makes no sense at all. Such is the topsy-turvy lifestyle of the islands.

While careening down the middle of the road (also customary) and flying around curves (on two bald tires), one terrified passenger faces the oncoming frightened face of another passenger. The cars whiz by with merely inches to spare. St Thomas is not a place where one can hang one's elbow on the window ledge. You can very well have your arm knocked off by an oncoming vehicle. Just like mom warned me as a kid. Most cars do not have right-side rear-view mirrors for this reason. Most were knocked off the first few weeks of ownership, especially because the streets are too narrow for many of the fat American cars.

Most tourist taxi drivers prefer to drive big ugly vans, with seating crammed to the maximum. No longer was it really a taxi service but rather a pricey bus business. The owners of the new-ish vans refuse to drive unless they were three-quarters full. And they drag hapless passengers through numerous stops before reaching their final destination.

Passengers are then charged the full private taxi rates, even though the system is in reality a temperamental bus service.

Indeed, St Thomas had a marginally functional public bus system. Unlike the taxi drivers, the buses are forced to stop only at the inconveniently placed bus stops. The convenient stops were all reserved for the illegally parked taxis.

Delilah loaded all the ice and shopping into the station wagon; it was at least ten years old. The kind once favored by the taxis that serviced the hotels, the airport, and the ship docks. These days, the tourist taxis were all vans. This gypsy with the station wagon worked mainly the locals, running errands.

Ready to deliver all the parcels quickly to the nearby marina, they pulled out of the illegal parking spot and into the street. And then the unthinkable happened.

The station wagon collided with an old yellow Toyota pulling into the lot. The gypsy jumped out, shaking his fists and yelling at the other driver. The other driver, a woman, got out and pointed to the minimal damage, saying it was nothing, The gypsy insisted it was something. The volume of their voices rose as they began talking in rapid West Indian lingo, shouting at each other.

Delilah got out to inspect and was shocked to find that it truly was minor, a little dent with a scratch on both cars. It blended in nicely with the rest of the rusty dents adorning both old, island cars.

A small crowd gathered including other gypsies waiting at the grocery store for fares.

Delilah asked another one to take her to the marina. She opened the back of the station wagon. Her driver yelled at her as she began removing her bags. He ran around, telling her she had to wait on him.

Delilah protested. Her ice was melting and her meat rotting in this ridiculous heat. She remembered to squeak her teeth loudly at him, to let him know she'd been around the island a time or two. The new gypsy was rooting for her.

Meanwhile, the Toyota owner sped out of the parking lot.

"You mudderscunt!" Screamed the gypsy, while shaking his fists in the air. He glared at Delilah. She glared right back.

"I have a sailboat waiting on me at the marina. Take me now, or I will ride with this mon. Either way, I have to go now!"

The poor driver reloaded her groceries. She got in the front seat. He hit the steering wheel muttering about the wreck and then put the car into gear, easing carefully out of the parking lot.

Delilah didn't say a word. The driver carried on a litany about the accident. It wasn't his fault. The lady driver should pay to repaint his entire station wagon. He rambled on, pulling into the marina.

She directed him to a spot close to the boat. They both got out. He opened the tailgate of the station wagon. Delilah removed as many grocery bags as she could carry, heading for the sailboat. The driver said that will be twelve dollars. He continued his recitation about the accident.

Delilah nodded her head. She kept walking toward the boat. Reaching the gangway, she hollered for Arnie.

Returned to the station wagon, where the taxi man waited with his hand outstretched.

"It wasn't my fault. D'at yellow Toyota had no business d'ere."

She grabbed up more bags and another block of ice.

"That will be twelve dollars."

Delilah nodded.

"Uh, hum."

She struggled with the heavy load up the gangway. Arnie was not aboard. She set the dripping ice on the sole of the cockpit. Her arms were sore.

She returned to the taxi. The gypsy was standing there with both hands stretched out.

"Twelve dollars. No, sir was not my fault. She done mash up my pretty station wagon."

Delilah bent over the tailgate, pulling out the case of ginger ale. She turned around, placing it on the man's arms.

He stood there astonished, as if she had just puked all over his shoes. Grabbing a box of canned soups, she set them atop the ginger ale case.

She carried the remaining two ice-blocks, walking over to the gangway. The hapless driver followed her with his load. He waited for her to climb aboard to set the ice down. He passed the two cases over to her.

They returned to the station wagon where the heavy lifeboat canister awaited. The taxi mon groaned, but he reluctantly helped Delilah with the canister. He even went all the way up the gangway with her to deposit it in the cockpit.

Delilah handed him fifteen dollars. He looked melancholy as he stared at the bills and mumbled that it was worth a lot more than that. He complained further about his mashed-up car. Delilah looked at the less-than-showroom-condition rust bucket. It made her smile, the irony of it all. Hell, it was the boat's money. She pulled out another five-dollar bill, wishing the gypsy a better afternoon.

He actually mumbled a thanks as he strolled towards his mashed-up car. Delilah stored the ice and provisions. Arnie came back with a bag full of marine parts. They wrestled the life raft canister to the foredeck, lashing it down in front of the mast. The rest of the afternoon was spent readying the vessel for offshore adventure.

At sunset, they left to go search for crew again. At The-Hole-In-The-Wall-Bar, they met Mac. He was on shore leave from a decrepit freighter. The first mate and cook had just jumped ship.

By Dear Miss Mermaid

Delilah was sort of interested; cooking would pay far better than this delivery. Perhaps she might go visit the freighter captain. Arnie ordered steaks for them. Their last meal in port, if all went well. He intoned that might have to leave without a third crewmember. Delilah told him to forget it. She wasn't going without a third member, and perhaps a fourth would even be nice. Arnie rolled his eyes. Mac was getting drunk.

Arnie left for the rest room, after finishing his New York strip. Delilah asked Mac to introduce her to the freighter captain. When Arnie returned, Delilah stood up, announcing she would be back in few minutes. She winked at Arnie, and then strolled out of the bar with Mac.

The freighter was tied up along the commercial wharf. It was the quintessential rustbucket in very sad shape. The galley proved to be a garbage bin with a mountain of pizza boxes and hamburger wrappers, interspersed with cockroaches. Mac showed her his cabin, which reeked of smelly sweat and mildew. He had been sleeping on a piece of moldy foam rubber that wasn't nearly large enough for the bunk. It was a pigsty. He showed her the cabin for the cook. It was even worse, with cracked paint, dirt and grime firmly affixed to every surface and did not have any foam at all on the bed.

"Well," Mac explained, "It is up to each crew member to furnish their cabin, you see."

After seeing the galley and accommodations, Delilah was not the least bit interested in taking the job, but she still suffered through the introduction to the captain who never took his eyes off her breasts. He invited Delilah up to his cabin for an intimate interview. Delilah could not scramble off the ship fast enough.

On the walk back to the bar, Delilah asked Mac if he would like to go sailing with her for a few days. He liked the idea. He had just been paid his month's wages. The captain was feeding them cold greasy take-out food while searching for a cook and a first mate. It was a kind of rotten ship. He could pack in minutes.

They sat down next to Arnie. Delilah winked at him.

"Mac would like to go sailing with us!"

"Terrific!"

Arnie's face lit up. He ordered the bartender to bring Mac another drink and turned and shook his hand.

"Welcome aboard!"

"I'm not sure. I'm thinking about it."

"Oh, Mac, it *will be fun!*"

Delilah winked at Arnie again. He nodded. Tiring of The-Hole-In-The-Wall, she suggested they go to Barnacle Bill's Bar, since it was Monday night. Lime Light night. Musicians from all over the island would pour in with their various instruments. The house band was on hand as were their instruments and sound equipment. Everyone who wanted to play would get a chance.

The trio ambled the few blocks over to the waterfront bar. Inside was a cacophony of noisy happy-hour conversation. Italian odors poured from the kitchen. The bar was nearly two deep.

Van Whalen was the master of ceremonies. He ran around with tiny reading glasses perched at the end of his nose, carrying a clipboard, making a list of the musicians as they came in.

A few minutes later, he lit up the stage, and then told a few jokes. Next he introduced a guitar player who sat down. He sang a mournful country tune, utilizing exactly three chords on the guitar.

They found a small table. Arnie ordered a round of drinks. Van Whalen introduced the upcoming act, a group of three teenage musicians. Frenchies form the North Side.

They had their own patois, different from the West Indians. This trio was rock and rollers. The singer, who could have been all of fifteen, stood there playing his guitar, a cap pulled low over his eyes as he stared only at his guitar and the microphone. The first song went off okay. The crowd gave a nice round of applause, asking for more. The musicians looked over to the emcee on the side of the stage. He nodded.

They warmed up and played really well. A few people graced the dance floor. The bartenders here knew how to hustle. Never stopping for anything, they made steady motions. Making drinks, taking money, asking for orders, watching the bar with radar precision for an empty cup, a questioning look.

The teen rock group finished another song to a round of applause. The host took over, thanking them. He introduced a tall West Indian woman along with her keyboard player who sat down at the lit keyboard and began playing a tune. The singer grabbed the microphone and walked back to the darkest part of the stage. She stood there in the dark, singing horribly out of tune. As she screeched on some of the higher notes, the crowd let out audible groans. The moment she finished, Van Whalen bounded across the stage with his house band in tow. Snatching the microphone from her, he thanked her as he hustled her off the stage.

The house band played a quick tune to liven things up before the unhappy crowd departed. Van Whalen introduced another musician who came and played with the house band. The dance floor swelled with dancers.

As the night wore on, the best musicians came in later. A cover charge was charged at the door unless you were a performer. Delilah had snuck in before by telling them she was a magician who planned to do an act as she patted her black nylon backpack. It worked. Another time she told them she was a visiting singer and they let her in since she wasn't carrying an instrument.

Arnie fetched another round. Between hiccups, Mac explained he'd never sailed but always wanted to.

A beefy young man came up and asked Delilah to dance. He wore a skintight tank top, and his tanned muscles seeming to bulge out of his broad handsome shoulders. His curly brown hair was trimmed immaculately as was his beard. His jeans were tight on his small hips, incongruously coupled with leather cowboy boots.

It turned out that he was light on his feet, an excellent dancer. His name was Chris. Delilah spent the rest of the evening dancing with him, occasionally stopping back at the bar for a shot of Jaegermeister, chased down with ice water.

While Delilah danced herself sober, Arnie plied Mac with alcohol, then pizza. Delilah took Chris over to the table and introduced everyone. They sat down and munched a piece of pizza.

Mac's eyes were now at half-mast. He barely managed to slump in his seat, appearing ready to slide out of it at any moment.

The harmonica player was wailing. The club had nearly gone silent as everyone turned to see who *this* guy was. Delilah and Chris got up to dance.At the end of the song, the club reverberated with claps, whoops and cheers. Chris asked Delilah if she wanted to go outside and smoke.

They weeded their way through the oppressive throng of noisy revelers then out the side door, where the air was cooler and not near as smoky. Unexpectedly, Chris grabbed Delilah and planted a lingering luscious kiss on her lips. She giggled when he pulled away. Taking her hand he escorted her to his car. They got in and rolled down the windows. He inserted the ignition key and turned it on so the cassette stereo could play. He pulled a small bag of pot out of his cowboy boot, and then reached around to his back pocket, producing a set of rolling papers. He began rolling the joint, while Delilah listened to the music.

When he finished rolling the joint, he turned to Delilah and kissed her again.

Then he straightened up, lit the joint, taking a long lazy inhale. He held his breath, wordlessly passing it over to Delilah. She took a long puff, watching Chris out of the corner of her eye as they listened to *Dark Side of The Moon.*

Some people walked through the parking lot laughing, yelling a hello to Chris. He let out a throaty giggle, hung his head out the window, joint still poised in one hand.

"Just getting some fresh air, mon!"

They finished the joint and necked to *Bolero*. Chris asked Delilah to come home with him. She told him she was sailing to Annapolis that night.

Chris sat bolt upright. She explained she'd probably be back in ten to fourteen days. He made her promise to look him up.

They returned to Barnacle Bill's, danced some more, and necked during the slow songs.

Around two a.m., all the lights came on, and the band shut down. Delilah and Chris headed out of the bar. A debauched Mac, wobbling on Arnie's arm, followed them. Mac carried on a litany of burps, belches and aromatic hiccups that caused them all to laugh. They crossed the parking lot to Chris's car. He volunteered to drive them to the marina, save them the struggle with Mac's ungainly gait.

"Hmm," said Arnie, as he poured Mac into the back seat of the tiny Honda two-door.

"Could you stop by the freighter docks? Mac here needs to pick up his bag, if you don't mind."

Chris didn't mind, as it would give him more time with Delilah, an interesting creature traveling with this Swiss guy with an accent and a drunk.

Setting out to sea, what a shame. He hoped she'd look him up when she was back on island.

At the *Caribe Moon* all four got out of the Honda to unload an unsteady Mac. Arnie struggled with him up the ship's ramp. He was a bit nervous boarding anther's ship, but on the other hand he didn't want to risk Mac falling overboard.

Chris leaned against the car's hood, pulling Delilah into his arms.

"Are you really sailing tonight?"

"Yes, I'm afraid so. We've been waiting for a third crew member, and well, um, looks like we have Mac now."

"You little pirate! I thought you were a mermaid!"

"I'm both! Haven't you noticed?"

"You look me up when you get back? Maybe we could go for dinner. Have you seen the island? I could show you around."

"I'd love that."

Arnie was leaning against the railing of the freighter. All was quiet. The deck was dimly lit by bulbs in glass jars covered with wire-mesh. He pretended not to watch the lovers below, but did so anyhow.

A few moments later, Mac came stumbling around the wheelhouse, dragging a hastily tied duffel bag with a dirty T-shirt and a pair of wrinkled pants flowing out of the top. He hesitated, swaying from side-to-side, and then he heaved the bag with a loud thump over the side of the freighter, narrowly missing the water. His bag landed on the wharf's edge, half-on-half-off the dirty cement.

Chris broke his embrace with Delilah, retrieved the bag and placed it in his trunk. Arnie assisted Mac down the gangway and stuffed him in the back seat. Chris drove them to the marina, *Yanni* playing on the tape player. Mac snored noisily. Chris kept one hand on the steering wheel, his other gently holding Delilah's.

At the marina it took three of them to unload an inebriated Mac. Arnie was holding him up, thanking Chris for the ride and assistance. Mac wobbled from side to side, taking an unsteady step forward. Before Arnie could react, Mac tripped over a dock cleat, falling head first into the murky waters.

Arnie and Chris pulled him back on the dock, laughing uproariously all the while. Mac stood there blinking his eyes uncertainly. "My hat!"

His red, Mount Gay baseball cap was floating away with a palm frond and a Styrofoam cup for company.

Chris said his last farewell and departed. Arnie managed to get Mac aboard and stuffed him into a shower. It did nothing to improve his drunkenness but at least the fishy-oily odor dissipated somewhat. Mac staggered out, a towel wrapped around his waist. Stretching out on the saloon's settee, he promptly passed out as his towel unfolded, falling to the floor. Delilah cast a sheet across his naked form.

Arnie and Delilah went on deck to finish preparations. Around three-thirty in the morning, they untied their lines, heading for the open ocean.

Arnie took the first watch, four to seven a.m. Delilah went below to sleep for three hours. Her watch dinged her at 6:55. Rubbing her eyes, she got up, used the head, and then poked her head in the cockpit.

"Morning, Arnie. Want some coffee, or something to eat?"

"No, I just want to sleep. Wake up Mac at ten a.m., see if he can steer the next shift."

They reviewed their course heading, and Arnie climbed into the aft cabin. Delilah was alone at the helm. She looked behind her. Jost Van Dyke (aka Goats Van Dyke) was fading on the horizon.

Even with only three hours of sleep, she felt refreshed. It was fun to command a yacht out at sea. She passed the morning humming to herself, steering, thinking about Chris. Would he really remember her in two weeks?

Around ten a.m. Mac stirred below. He sat up on the bunk, rubbing his head and moaning. He opened his bloodshot eyes. He looked all around him. A shaft of sunlight blinded him from the companionway. He could see a silhouette sitting at the wheel.

The night before was beginning to come back to him in bits and pieces. He stood up, and then fell down. The ship was leaning! Wait. This was not his ship. This was a small sailboat. My God. How did he end up here?

"Good morning Mac!"

The voice sounded vaguely familiar. That chick. The one he had been hitting on in the bar. She was with some guy with an accent. Sailing. He agreed to go sailing. Ah, yes. All was clear.

"Can you take the helm? I'll make some coffee."

Mac found his shorts in the floor, slid them on then climbed out into the cockpit and blinked a few times.

"Take the what?"

"Here, take the wheel. Keep it on oh-one-oh. North," she tapped the compass.

Mac looked all around him. Miles of ocean.

"When do we get back to St. Thomas?"

"In about two weeks, maybe ten days."

"What? I'm supposed to sail on *Caribe Moon* tomorrow!"

"Naw, Mac. You jumped ship. You're sailing to Annapolis with us."

"I jumped ship?"

"Yep. Your duffel bag is on the forward bunk in case you want to change. I'll take the helm back when the coffee is ready."

"Could you grab me a beer, please?"

"We don't have any beer."

"Okay, rum then."

"No rum."

"What do you have then?"

"Coffee, tea, water, juice, ginger ale. Take your pick."

"When do we stop next?"

"In about ten or so days."

"You've *got* to be kidding."

"Nope."

"Take me back to St Thomas. I thought we were just going to sail *for the day*."

"Can't."

"We're signed on to deliver this boat to Annapolis."

"Oh my God. I don't believe this. I *need* a beer!"

"Sorry. Here, I'll take the wheel while you finish getting dressed. Come back up when you're done, it's your shift until two p.m."

"My *shift*?"

"Yeah, we each steer three hours, off six-hours. It's your turn. Then Arnie will take over at two and I'll be back at five."

Mac shook his head from side-to-side. He scanned the horizon.

"Hey, is that Florida?"

"No, it's Puerto Rico."

Groan. Sigh. Mac retreated below to change into his clothes. He returned with black coffee and a cigarette, which sent him into a fit of coughs. He took the wheel.

"See you later, Mac. Knock three times if you run into any trouble.

"What kind of trouble?"

"You know, pirates and stuff."

"Pirates!"

"Just kidding. Keep a look out for other boats and stay out of their way. Keep us on oh-one-oh."

For the next few days, they sailed in pleasant weather, making good time. Arnie and Delilah argued about the navigation lights at night. He wanted to save power by not using them. Delilah wanted to obey the law of the seas and display them so they could be seen. On her watch, she ran with the lights, on his they ran without them. It made her nervous, to know she was sleeping below on an unlit boat.

In the rolling galley, they managed to make some food from time to time. Delilah was grateful for the ginger ale and saltine crackers. It was all she felt like eating the first few days.

Their electronics were limited to depth sounder (useless this far offshore), wind indicator, boat speed, and compass. Soon they were out of VHF radio range, no longer able to obtain weather reports. Whenever they saw another ship, they would try to hail them on the radio, to see if they had a weather fax. No one ever answered.

Arnie wanted them to keep the radio off between calls, to conserve the batteries. If anyone ever tried to hail them, they knew not of it. What they also did not know was that they were heading straight into a gale. The winds were gusting up to sixty miles an hour just north of them. Delilah was alone on the deck. It was dark, save for the tiny navigation lights atop the mast. The wind was freshening, the boat becoming harder to steer. Delilah's arms began to ache two hours into her shift.

Previously Arnie had complained that the centerboard had fallen off while the boat was in a bareboat charter. Rather than replace it, the company had fiberglassed over it, giving it a much shorter keel. The rig was badly tuned and this resulted in excessive weather helm.

To make matters even worse, some egotistical owner who fancied himself a racer had put this ridiculous five-foot wheel on the small boat. It was the most uncomfortable thing to handle.

Climbing back and forth around the massive wheel was tricky, as the boat lay over nearly on her ear, beating herself windward. Wearing a harness around her shoulders and waist, with a line hooked to a D-ring then tied to the wheelbase, Delilah was attached to the boat should the wind and waves try to wrench her out to sea.

Delilah was tired. Her arms hurt. She'd be grateful for a dry bunk in the next hour.

At four a.m. that night, Mac took the helm. Delilah dozed off into an exhausted slumber on the starboard side of the saloon. A half-hour later, Delilah was rudely awakened by a tremendous bang. She landed with a dull thud on the saloon floor. Climbing up, she noticed the boat was leaning to port!

Delilah opened the companionway and went on deck. Mac was singing at the top of his lungs.

"*She was a fine lass, a fine lass was she...*" He was banging on the wheel with his coffee spoon. The boat had jibed and now they were backwinded.

Delilah got him back on course. She went below to lie down, when he jibed them again. This time, Arnie came up and tied down the boom with a makeshift boom-preventer.

He rehearsed with Mac how to steer the boat. Mac seemed to be lost in another world. Perhaps the DT's had gotten to him finally. Arnie started up the engine; they needed to charge the battery anyway. It would make it easier for Mac to steer.

Delilah dropped off to sleep immediately, ignoring the whine of the diesel. She was too tired to think. Dreamy thoughts of being at the beach, listening to the waves splash gently on shore drifted through her lethargic brain. Opening one eye, reality began to permeate her sleepy consciousness; the floorboards were awash! The cabin was taking on water.

Splashing out of her bunk, she went aft to wake up a grouchy Arnie. He dug around the bilge looking for the automatic pump. She went up top to start pumping with the manual pump located in the cockpit. Inserting the long handle, she bobbed up and down, but only sad gasps greeted her efforts. The manual pump was broken or clogged or both.

"Get the buckets!" Arnie yelled from below.

She retrieved a three and a five-gallon bucket from the cockpit locker. Arnie and Delilah began the bucket brigade, trying to make a dent in the seemingly endless waterfall entering the cabin.

Mac continued singing at the wheel, steering wildly. Arnie "accidentally" threw a bucket of bilge water right at Mac. He blinked his eyes, rubbed his face, continuing to sing. He was terrible, and hopelessly out of tune.

Eventually their interior sea receded to a mere trickle. Arnie searched the boat, speculating the waves coming over the bow were finding an unknown hole to pour in. To match the rate at which it was coming in, they devised a system at watch changes for each crew to bail out the bilge.

Already the interior of the boat was starting to take on an odor of its own, as their sweaty salt-sprayed clothes piled up. They could not open any hatches to air the place out; the seas were far to rough. Even the companionway had to be closed up whenever it rained, making it miserably hot down below.

In the morning, Arnie took the bimini down, storing it below. Delilah preferred the shade. Arnie was adamant it would speed up their course.

That afternoon, while Delilah was at the helm, the seas built up to twenty-foot waves. They sure looked taller than their mast as the sleigh ride began. Sailing up each wave, *Shanghai* crested, then surfed down into the trough. The sky darkened. The storm brewed. Soon a pelting rain was upon them. Delilah was really cold. Unable to leave the wheel, she banged furiously on the cockpit with the winch hammer.

Arnie woke up, tossing her foul weather gear and a snorkel mask out into the cockpit. Delilah cursed him for taking down the bimini. She steered, soaked to the bone and freezing. The rain was hitting her face so hard that she was forced to wear the snorkel mask.

When Mac peaked out before his watch, it was still pouring rain. He screamed when he saw the apparition in the cockpit. The thing was dressed head-to-toe in a red foul-weather jumpsuit. A snorkel mask stuck out from a tightly laced red hood. Where its mouth should have been, a hose stuck out (the snorkel tube.) Delilah pulled off the mask and tossed it at Mac.

"Put on your foul-weather gear!"

"My what?"

"Oh, Jesus! Get a garbage bag then, and cut out a neck and arms. Wear that!"

When Mac returned, Delilah went below, undressing in the shower. She cut on the water to rinse off, which woke Arnie up. He yelled at her not to waste any. She cursed him. He went back to sleep. Mac banged the wheel with his coffee spoon, singing off key.

Coming out of the shower, she noticed the floorboards were awash again. She bailed out about thirty gallons of water with the buckets. She was exhausted. She opened up the refrigerator to get some juice. The ice had given out and a rank smell permeated the air. She closed the contraption and settled for some saltine crackers and a warm ginger ale. She tried to lie on the starboard saloon bunk. It smelled like Mac. She envied Arnie in the aft cabin, in the huge bunk, nice and comfy.

The ridiculous three-on and six-off shift was taking its toll. Their eyes darkened, and their faces appeared strained and fatigued. Fighting that five-foot wheel with an inadequate keel made a terrible weather helm, leaving them all very sore after each watch.

Delilah implored Arnie to change to two on and four off. Let their bodies get some semblance of a schedule for sleeping and working He was adamant they keep up the nine-hour rotating watch.

On Monday, Delilah was at the helm from 6 a.m. to 9 a.m., and 3 'til 6 p.m. On Tuesday her watches were midnight to 3 a.m., 9 a.m. to noon, and 6 'til 9 p.m. Wednesday, her watches were 3 till 6 a.m., then noon till 3 p.m., and 9 to midnight. The schedule then repeated. Her body clock was not adapting at all. Everyone's tempers were now a bit short. All three were exhausted.

Delilah was on the midnight-to-three watch when all hell broke loose. It was pitch black, rain poured, the sky thundered, and visibility decreased drastically. The winds gusted to forty miles an hour and up. Delilah was tethered to the steering pedestal with her safety harness.

She always had to put Mac's on for him when he came on watch. He was like a child in a man's body. The last watch he had been hallucinating pretty heavily, yelling about penguins and polar bears. His coffee spoon became his pacifier. He sucked on it, banged the wheel with it while singing, and momentarily cried when he dropped it nearly out of reach.

Up on deck, Delilah was cold, wet and scared. The boat had become impossible to steer. She fought to stay on their intended course, the boat zigzagging wildly. Rain poured in sheets. Salty waves broke across the deck. Shanghai was grossly over-canvassed for the conditions. In exasperation, Delilah banged on the cockpit sole with the winch handle. Arnie would be sleeping down below in the aft cabin.

She stared straight ahead at the companionway boards, waiting for them to open. Nothing. She banged harder. A few moments later, an angry Arnie pulled open the companionway hatch. Rain battered his face. He leaned back inside, yelling at Delilah, to be heard above the cacophony of the raging storm.

"What?"

Delilah took out the snorkel mouthpiece.

"Come reef the main, please!" The rain was hitting her facemask so hard, that she just sort of saw Arnie as a fuzzy ever-changing mosaic.

"It doesn't need reefing. We'll lose speed."

"Yes it does! It's gusting like crazy out here. We're gonna get knocked down! There's too much sail up, Arnie!"

He stuck his head out, turning around to look up at the mainsail. Rain cascaded over his face and through his hair. He ducked back inside.

"It's fine! We'll make better time this way."

He shut the hatch. Case closed.

Delilah banged the winch handle twice again, yelling as loud as she could at the closed companionway.

"Arnie! It's impossible to stay on course!"

"Start the engine, then!"

As it turned out, it was a good thing Arnie *did* shut the hatch. The rainstorm raged, and the wind howled. Suddenly their world went topsy-turvy. As Shanghai laid down broad side, and her rudder came out of the water. The wheel spun uncontrollably, knocking Delilah's hands off. She was thrown violently over to the side, splashing half-in and half-out of the ocean. The safety harness strapped over her foul-weather gear was still tethered, preventing the ocean from snatching her away in the dark of night.

Screaming herself hoarse, she managed to clamor out of the water. *Shanghai* seemed to slow down; Delilah crawled to the helmsman's seat. *Shanghai* abruptly righted herself, crossed over the wind and gibed, nearly laying the sails in the water. The wheel spun madly out of control, the rudder slamming back and fourth. The boat shuddered with each bang.

Delilah started the diesel, regaining control of the wheel. The sails flapped noisily making a deafening racket. Rain and waves crashed across the deck.

Visibility was less than the thirty-six foot length of the boat. Grasping the wheel with all her might, Delilah headed the boat into the wind.

Arnie scrambled up on deck to reef the mainsail. There was a huge tear across the foot of the sail. Fortuitously, it was below the reef points Arnie managed to tie in. He crab-crawled back to the cockpit. Delilah slowly turned the wheel until they were back on course. The boat heeled over, beating into the wind. Delilah was shaking like a palm frond in a hurricane, adrenaline hotwiring her heart.

Arnie stood drenched in the cockpit looking up at the sails. Delilah followed his gaze. All the mainsail batten pockets were ripped open, their battens gone, save for one that was lying on the deck. Delilah pointed it out to Arnie. He scrambled forward to retrieve it. A wave washed over the deck, snatching the batten away. He cursed the sea, the weather, the boat, and the owner. Then he went below, bailed out the bilge, cursing the weather for making him loose precious sleep.

Delilah left the engine on. She breathed deeply, staring at the lit compass, then at her hands gripping the stainless steel curve of the wheel.

She prayed. Then she thought back to the idyllic first few days when the weather, wind and waves were quite favorable, Arnie wasn't so cranky and Mac not as crazy. Ah, the life offshore is full of surprises. She took a long deep breath, vowing to sail *Shanghai* to Annapolis, and arrive alive, mission accomplished. Cheat death one more time.

Sailing offshore is sheer boredom relieved by moments of sheer terror.

Delilah wasn't bored on this trip, just exhausted. Hunger pangs toiled with her thoughts for a while. Fixing food was such a chore in this chaotic sea. She'd long since lost her appetite, but felt weak. For the last few days she'd only had coffee at the beginning of her watch, then saltines and Ginger Ale afterwards, slurping and munching in her bunk.

Tonight, she was plenty busy just trying to hold onto the massive wheel while rain pelted her. She used her feet to help steer; it made her feel a tad more secure. Besides, as quick as the cockpit would drain itself of water, another wave coupled with the torrential rain would fill it again. Her wool socks were soaked, but warm on her bootless feet.

When her watch was over, her body was weary but her brain was wide awake, still on full alert. Mac opened the companionway to change watches with her. He was wearing her pink flow- ered shower cap, secured by a snorkel mask. His neck disappeared into a custom-cut heavy-duty silver garbage bag.

He handed her a mug of hot chocolate. Steering with her feet, she cupped it in both hands as the rainwater threatened to overfill it. She took a sip with her teeth chattering against the cup. Then she drank the entire mug in one fell swoop.

Mac took over the wheel. She scrambled down below. Standing in the shower stall, she undressed. There was hardly anywhere to hang up her gear; the whole boat was reeking of moldy smelling towels and sweaty clothes. She lied down amidships in the starboard bunk. It was overly warm in the cabin from the engine heat. No hatches were open because of the gale.

Still, she could hear Mac up on deck. He began to sing in a deep voice:

She had a dark and a roving eye,
and her hair hung down in ring-e-lets;
She was a nice girl, a proper girl,
but one of the roving kind!!

As I went out one evening, upon a night's career,
I spied a lofty clipper ship,
And to her I did steer,
I hoisted up my signal, which she did quickly view,
And when I had my bunting up,
She immediately hove to!

She had a dark and a roving eye,
and her hair hung down in ring-e-lets;

She was a nice girl, a proper girl,
but one of the roving kind!!

Excuse me sir, she said to me, for being out so late,
For if my parents knew of it,
then sad would be my fate,
My father is a minister, a true a noble man;
My mother is a reverend, I do the best I can!

She had a dark and a roving eye,
and her hair hung down in ring-e-lets;
She was a nice girl, a proper girl,
but one of the roving kind!!

I took her to a tavern, and treated her to wine,
For little did I realize, she was of the roving kind,
I handled her, I dandled her,
but much to my surprise,
She was nothing but an old pirate ship,
Done up in a disguise!

She had a dark and a roving eye,
and her hair hung down in ring-e-lets;
She was a nice girl, a proper girl,
but one of the roving kind!!

So gather round, ye sailor men,
who sail upon the sea
and gather round, ye 'prentice lads,
come take a tip from me;

Beware of them they're fire ships;
they'll be the ruin of you,
'Twas there I had my mizzen sprung,
my strong box broken through!

She had a dark and a roving eye,
and her hair hung down in ring-e-lets;
She was a nice girl, a proper girl,
but one of the roving kind!!

Delilah was just drifting off to sleep when
Mac yanked her out of her reverie by screaming
at the very top of his lungs so loud it was clearly
heard above the noise of the gale and the whine
of the diesel.

"All together now!"

She had a dark and a roving eye,
and her hair hung down in ring-e-lets;
She was a nice girl, a proper girl,
but one of the roving kind!!

"Big finish now! Sing it!" Mac yelled then
sang quite loudly while the ship drove wildly in
his inexperienced hands:

B-U-U-U-U-U-T...
O-N-N-N-N-N-E
OF THE
R-O-O-O-O-O-O-V-I-N-G
K-I-I-I-I-I-N-D !

As Delilah drifted off to sleep, she could hear Mac conversing with himself. First he would speak in a deep male voice, then answer in a falsetto voice.

"How was that, me pirate, Lady Rose?"

"Oh, Finn, that was wonderful!"

"Have a drink, lassie, Pusser's Blue, the best!"

"Why thank you, Finn."

Mac loudly banged his coffee spoon on the stainless steel steering pedestal.

"Cheers, Lady Rose!"

"Oh, Finn, my darling, sing me another, please!"

"Ah, for you, anytime lass. Here's a sweet and sad one for you!"

Back in his deep voice, he sang:

Paddy met her in Venezuela,
With a basket on her head.
And if she knew others she did not say,
But Paddy knew she'd do to pass away,

To pass away the time in Venezuela.
To pass away the time in Venezuela.
Paddy bought her a beautiful silken scarf of blue.
A beautiful scarf of blue.

And when 'twas time for her ship to go to sea…
her ship away to sea,
and she was taking leave of her,
she said, Cheer up, there always be….

Delilah dozed on and off, aware of the noises around her. She heard Arnie start bailing the bilge by bucket prior to his watch. He opened the companionway hatch to toss the bucket into the cockpit sole; it would drain aft from there. She gulped in the fresh air that filled the cabin. She dozed off again, knowing she would take over the helm again in a mere three hours.

An hour or so later, she awoke to a terrible feeling. She sat up on the yawing bunk, coughing in spasms and fits. She seemed too hot, the air so thick. Staggering across the sloping floor, she threw open the sliding hatch.

A cloud of smoke turned to dark mist around her. The rain pelted her face and the stairs.

"Close the hatch, Delilah!"

A luminous dark cloud billowed out from the companionway; for a moment, Arnie thought he was hallucinating. Delilah continued to gulp for air and cough, almost choking on the rainwater, but it felt so good, even though her T-shirt was now soaked through.

"Grab the wheel!" screamed Arnie, as he leapt down below to check on the engine.

Black clouds of smoke poured out into the rainy night. Delilah tried to focus on the compass and steer. Her shirt was glued to her skin, but she seemed not to feel it.

The diesel went silent. Arnie had shut off the fuel supply. He roused Mac, who stumbled outside coughing wildly.

Catching his breath, he complained.

"The smog in L.A. is especially lethal this year!"

Arnie ignored him.

"The exhaust hose has broken off the engine. I'm going back down below to try to fix it with duct tape, if you can finish my shift, Delilah."

"Pass me my foul weather gear, then."

Back on watch, she concentrated on the approaching sunrise. The storm had abated some, the rain only intermittent now. The skies actually seemed to be clearing.

Mac came up for his watch. Delilah went down below. Sunlight filtered through the plastic hatches. The entire interior of the boat was caked in thick black soot. Foot tracks could be seen across the floor.

Towels and clothes that were draped from the handholds above in hopes of drying out were all a dingy gray. It was disgusting. The vessel looked like a refugee ship from the war with everything a battleship gray.

The crew was far too exhausted and taxed from the grueling watch schedule to do any cleaning. Delilah cleared a small spot in the galley to make some peanut-butter crackers. She ate her fill while making a stack for Mac.

The rain had stopped; they were able to keep the sliding hatch open above the companionway. The other hatches had to remain closed, as on this tack, the waves still splashed over the bow, running across the closed hatches. Unceremoniously, they leaked below after each wave, dripping into the putrid cabin.

Delilah bailed out the nasty bilge by bucketfuls then wearily laid down on the filthy bunk. Mac was silently steering up top, no longer singing. Arnie was fast asleep. The wind and waves were quite pleasant. All was quiet. The engine was off, what little fuel they had left was being conserved for coming into port. They expected to site land anytime.

Towards the end of Mac's watch, Arnie got up, making coffee while gulping down cold Dinty Moore stew, his spoon frantically scraping the inside of the can so as not to miss a morsel.

"Land ho! Land ho!"

Mac banged his coffee spoon loudly on the pedestal, waking up Delilah. Arnie threw the can in the garbage, grabbed his sextant then went up on deck.

For several minutes he sat there taking sightings and bearings. Back down below, he consulted the chart with a pencil. Making a few notes, he came back into the cockpit to announce the new course heading.

He estimated their arrival at the marina by sunset. Delilah crawled into the cockpit to get a glimpse of the land. Only miles of ocean had greeted her the past ten-and-a-half days. She looked forward to a decent shower and some clean clothes, as neither were now available on the boat. (Delilah learned later that they had plenty of water and that Arnie had lied to them.)

She stunk. Arnie and Mac had given up shaving and both looked a bit scraggly, neither having combed their dirty hair lately. Everyone wore dingy gray salt-encrusted smelly clothes. The New England autumn was far too cold to run around naked, which Delilah would have preferred over the filthy clothing. Her hair was tied in a French braid that was showing signs of wear.

"I'm going to eat a steak!"

"I want a cheeseburger with grilled onions!"

"I want an all-you-can-graze salad bar!"

"And an icy cold Heineken!"

"And a rum and coke!"

"And fresh orange juice!"

Like three children, they spent the day happily sharing their planned menus ashore, as they speculated where the nearest laundromat was. No one ate all day, saving up for their food orgy ashore.

Each took turns trying to clean their appearance up, but the gray sooty clothes still looked like a chimneysweepers' clothing. The wind freshened, and the jib split right down the middle. Arnie tried to furl it in, but it hung loosely in folds at the forestay, looking quite ratty as threads blew in the wind. The engine was chugging along modestly as they came into the marina. The VHF still worked, and Arnie summoned help for docking.

The marina they had been instructed to deliver to was the yacht club. The dockhands came out in matching uniforms, staring at the trio oddly. Their boat was a mess and the crew looked downright frightful.

The pair hastily cleated them off and then skedaddled down the dock as if in an urgent hurry, whispering to each other as they glanced over their shoulders at the motley sea drenched crew.

Anxious to try their sea legs on the dock, they gleefully stepped ashore to terra firma. Knowing they were a tad underdressed for the ritzy yacht club, they found a bar and restaurant that Arnie had been to before.

They ordered up drinks and a mountain of food. They talked of airline tickets and dirty laundry. Delilah and Mac were relived to discover that cleaning up the filthy yacht was not part of the delivery contract. Arnie explained that the boat was coming up to Annapolis for a major refit; there'd just be *more* to refit now. It wasn't as if they had abused the boat in any way, but rather they had been handed a shitty boat to start with. Arnie had kept the impending refit a secret.

Delilah silently fumed. If she had known this boat was due for a refit, then she might have looked at the delivery job with more of a skeptical eye. It had been a rather harrowing trip at times. Forgetting that, she concentrated on the food as the waitress layered the table with a Caesars' salad, oysters Rockefeller, shrimp cocktail, pepperoni pizza, garlic toast, a huge T-bone steak with baked potato topped with melted butter and sour cream, two cheeseburgers with grilled onions, an order of French fries and onion rings, with another side of coleslaw.

The table was practically overflowing as the crew dug in heartily amidst stares from other diners. Unable to eat the entire mountain of food, they packed the rest up to go and headed back for the boat.

Arnie took off with all their laundry to see about having it washed. Mac went looking for a store to buy more beer. Delilah fell into an exhausted slumber at 8 p.m.

When she awoke, it was two o'clock in the afternoon! To clear her head, she took a luxuriating showier, then wrapped up in a sooty towel. Arnie climbed aboard, all smiles, carrying three bags of laundry. He had showered and shaved, his hair was neatly combed and tied back in a loose ponytail. Delilah changed quickly and then began packing her sea bag.

"I've got another delivery. It goes to Florida. Leaving tomorrow. Want to go, Delilah?"

Delilah gave Arnie her best evil eye, coldly staring at him.

"I'd like to get paid for this trip first, please."

"Sure, no problem."

He opened his wallet and counted out her meager pay. Delilah mentally did the calculation in her head, it worked out to about fifty-cents an hour. Her ticket coupon was tucked away with her passport.

Arnie gave her his sexiest come-hither smile.

"Well, want to sail to Florida?"

"No, Arnie, I do not want to do anymore deliveries with you. You're a very nice person, but your judgment in a vessel's seaworthiness is much to be desired."

"Oh, darling, all the boats are that way, people always wanting them to be fixed somewhere else. This boat we just brought in is going to the boat yard for a complete refit; it just came out of the charter fleet. Now, this upcoming one, it's in better shape, but they want it fixed in Florida cause the owner lives there in the winter, you see. Come on, you're good crew, I like the way you handle things so well under stress."

Before Delilah could muster a reply, she spied a taxi dropping some people off at the end of the dock.

"Hey! Taxi!"

"Wait for me!"

She gave Arnie a big hug and hoisted her bag over her shoulder.

"See you later, Arnie. I'm going to fly standby. It's too cold this far north!"

She started down the dock towards the waiting car.

"You're missing out on a good career at boat delivery!"

Delilah wondered if was really so great after all. She returned to St Thomas, finding a charter boat to crew on for the winter season. Periodically, she'd run into Arnie, St Thomas was a major trans-shipment port for delivery captains.

Each time she saw him, he had wracked up a few thousand more ocean miles. One evening, Delilah heard her name called by a familiar voice. She turned around, but what she saw was not the Arnie she knew.

His face was a ragged crater of scabs and scars with angry red welts. Skin was peeling off his nose in great hunks.

"What happened to you?!"

"Oh..."

He waved his hand casually, as if to dismiss the subject as trivial.

"On this last delivery, we had a little explosion, no big deal. This will all heal up."

He looked hideous, even when he smiled and winked at her.

"By the way, I'm sailing for France tomorrow and need one more crew, Delilah..."

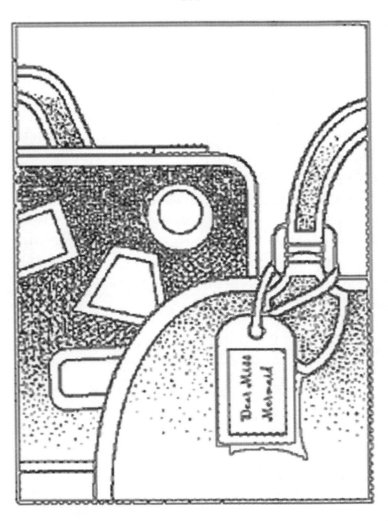

Travels of My Luggage

When I first came to the British Virgin Islands about 1980 or so, it was on a fluke. I had won a writing contest that gave me no money but a pile of gifts including a one-week trip for two aboard a Windjammer Tall Ship in the BVI. I had one year to use this gift. I was going to surprise my boyfriend with the trip as a gift for his birthday. I already had cheap airfare lined up, and the cruise tickets were free.

Just before my proposed trip, my boyfriend and I broke up. So I called the company and asked if my prize could be converted to two weeks for one, and they said yes—if they could give me a female shipmate to share my cabin. That sounded fine to me. I ran into my old boyfriend and had fun telling him I couldn't talk because I had to run pack for two weeks in the Caribbean.

I flew into St Thomas, and friends brought me to West End by private boat. An old rusty beat-up taxi, a Chevrolet Vega, picked me up. I had hours to kill before I could board the tall ship in Road Harbor, so the taxi *mon* took me on a tour of the BVI. Well, as best as he could! At one point, we started up Joe's Hill and that little Vega wouldn't make it, so we had to turn around and go back to Road Town. Later in the day, we hit a pothole and part of his fender fell off. We stopped to retrieve it.

He took me to eat at the Roti Palace, and I felt like I was in someone's home kitchen instead of a restaurant. At that time, there was very little car traffic on Tortola. Most folks drove beat-up old jeeps. I don't recall seeing any new cars anywhere. The taxis were beat-up too, a few were vans.

I boarded the ship by taking the ship's launch out to the anchorage. They made me leave my luggage on the dock with a pile of others. They promised they would make a special luggage run and fetch all of the luggage. Somehow between dock and ship, my luggage was lost. So I had two glorious weeks in the BVI with no luggage!

My luggage took on a life and tour of its own. While we sailed from harbor to harbor, my luggage did likewise, although to different harbors or at different times. It tended to land at places a day or two after I had left. And it visited a few ports where I never went.

At that time, there were only a handful of Moorings bareboats around. There were virtually no marinas; even West End had not been developed yet. There weren't even any mooring balls anywhere. We all had to anchor the old fashioned way.

One day I took a tour to Sage Mountain with other sail guests, and we ended up in a van with no brakes. "Don't worry, be happy," the driver would tell us as we snaked down the awful mountain roads as he used his hand brake to slow the van. I was in the front seat, and he laughed at me for looking for the seat belt. He claimed he was getting his brakes fixed one day soon—as if that would help us.

Jost Van Dyke didn't have electricity then, but Foxy entertained us just the same. At night he ran this old noisy generator to make lights and chill the freezers full of beer. Blender drinks were never served during daytime, because the generator wasn't used during daylight. The beers were iced in freezers from the night before. At that time Foxy's was just a shack. We had to pee in the woods. A few years later when I visited Foxy, I saw he had caved in and built an outhouse for the ladies. It was thatched on four sides, with no roof. The sign on the door read: "Ladies only! Men take a hike!"

At Salt Island, the crew took huge boxes of fresh vegetables and fruits to the then six residents living there. We toured the island and learned all about the Wreck of the Rhone, Six Men on a Dead Man's Chest, and how salt was made from the salt ponds.

At Norman Island we anchored out, the stern of the ship tied to a huge rock while we snorkeled right off the boat at the caves. We fed the fish stale crackers and they swarmed around us.

At the Baths in Virgin Gorda, we were the only visitors. I climbed the great rocks and took a bad fall and slid down, leaving a great deal of my belly skin on the huge boulder.

My luggage continued to be sighted but still eluded me. At Cane Garden Bay we anchored outside the harbor, just beyond the reef. Only three other boats were in the harbor. Our passenger manifest of 64 seemed like an invasion to this quaint seaside community. A Fungi Band played at Stanley's, and we danced on the beach that night.

A Fungi band is made up of mostly homemade instruments, ballads are song and the beat is for dancing.

Another night about 40 of us singles dragged our mattresses up topside and slept on the deck instead of our cabins. The mattresses were placed next to each other, forming a huge solitary bed. That was before the AIDS scare, and you can well imagine, it got pretty wild on deck in the wee hours of the morning. For some reason, this particular charter was about two-thirds singles and one-third couples; maybe because of the ship's willingness to assign you a cabin-mate if you were traveling alone.

My luggage continued on its own odyssey around the BVI. Apparently it had become lost that first day because it began raining as we boarded the ship. There were two piles of luggage on the dock, one pile destined for our ship and one for Virgin Gorda by ferry. Customs and Immigration ran out and dragged all the luggage under cover to protect it from the sudden downpour. My luggage was inadvertently tossed in the Virgin Gorda pile and sailed there without me.

When our tall ship arrived at Virgin Gorda a few days later, we were told my luggage had arrived and been sent back to Road Town on Tortola. At another point along the way, we were in Peter Island, and the launch ran over and fetched my luggage and brought it back. However, the contents were inexplicably covered in oil and were thus useless to me. There being no laundry facilities on the ship, the crew sent my luggage back to Road Town and to the laundry for me.

One night the ship had a Toga party, and we all wore out bed sheets to dinner on deck. It was a BBQ buffet. One man fetched his plate in one hand and his drink in his other. He decided it was too windy to dine topside, so he walked down the steep stairway to the dining saloon below. A gust of wind came by about the time his only knot gave way, and we heard this scream and were treated to the sight of a naked man with BBQ in one hand and a rum punch in the other looking forlornly at his sheet billowing out to sea.

He was quite a sight as he tried to cover his privates with first his plate and then his rum punch, while the rest of us roared with laughter. Finally he set his things down and took off running for his cabin to fetch a new sheet. He ran into the stewardess below deck, who knew nothing of this wardrobe malfunction, and she let out a shrill scream, which had us all in stitches.

Eventually we stopped back in Road Town, and I walked to the laundry to get my luggage, but alas! They had sent my stuff out to yet another boat, and that boat was God knows where.

I got back on the ship, still no luggage, and now I was into week two. At some point my luggage was returned to the laundry and eventually traveled by various ferries and taxis until it was returned to me on day 13, the last day of my first cruise in the BVI.

Lost luggage continued to plague me over the years. I would carefully label it and label its final destination, but it just never seemed to travel with me.

Once I flew out of Miami and went to Brazil for three weeks. My luggage went to St Thomas but they never shipped my luggage back, they just kept it and kept it and kept it. Finally about six weeks later, I found myself in St Thomas and inquired about my errant luggage. Sure enough, it was locked up in storage. Customs demanded to know what I had in it, and I said I had no idea, as I hadn't seen the bag in six weeks! No telling WHAT was in it.

They opened it up, dumped it out and asked me if it was mine. I shrugged my shoulders and said "Yep, looks like my stuff all right." There were a few things missing, but I hardly cared.

Another time, after I was crewing professionally, I moved off of a ship and was waiting for my then boyfriend to fetch me in Red Hook, St. Thomas. I turned my back to make a phone call, and when I turned back around a few minutes later, my luggage had vanished. I was speechless. I never heard a thing behind me!

About a week later, I got a phone call from the ship, as someone had found my luggage and wanted to return it to me. They claimed they found it halfway across the island in a dumpster and thought it looked too nice, so they rummaged through it and found my ship's discharge papers and called them. Meanwhile the ship offered me a job back on board, and I took it. My bag appeared, although missing a few items again.

I now travel with carry-on luggage only. I have given up checking my luggage. A while back I was traveling for two weeks, and my friend stopped by to drive me to the airport. She picked up my carry-on bag and said, "Wow this is light! I'll carry this, and you carry the rest."

When we reached her car, she noticed I wasn't carrying anything and she asked, "Where is your luggage?"

"You are holding it!" I told her.

She said, "No way! This is much too light, like it's only half full."

"Yep, I wanted to leave room for shopping..."

She snorted and shook her head and said, "I thought you were going on vacation for two weeks!"

"Yep, that's why I packed at all! I packed a sarong, a pair of shorts, a shirt, a bathing suit, clean undies, plus the clothes I am wearing, and then I may shop some. Mother Teresa traveled around the world with only three outfits—one to wear, one to wash, and one to spare, and that works for me!"

And that put an end to my lost luggage.

Come Blow Away My Hurricane Blues

In the fall of 1995, Hurricane Luis slammed into the U.S. Virgin Islands. The damage was not devastating for most, though a few people lost their roofs or their boats. Losing a vessel is especially a hardship for those that live aboard full time, without a land home anywhere. Residents picked up the scattered pieces, beginning to put their lives back together. Lo and behold, a mere ten days later, about the time all were breathing a sigh a relief, along came hurricane Marilyn with devastating consequences.

A few people were killed, quite a few were missing, most staying aboard their sailboats rather than ashore, a foolish choice that cost some, their lives. A great deal of property was lost. Roofs had blown completely away and sometimes the walls as well. Furniture was destroyed, personal belongings strewn from leafless trees and pathetic brown shrubbery, the green leaves having been completely blown away. Tourism ground to an abrupt halt. The few remaining tourists camped out at the airport, waiting for the first flight to take them away from this nightmare.

Utility poles had toppled across the roads, the lines now lifeless. Because the police are unable to control crime in a non-hurricane situation, a ridiculous curfew was imposed at sunset, in the US Virgin Islands, making already miserable lives more miserable. Many folks went home to nothing. I will explain what that nothing meant for many hurricane victims.

No roof.
No electricity.
No running water.
No telephone.
No cable TV.
No refrigeration.
No cooking.
No food.
No furniture.
No walls.
No job.
No money.
No car.
No fans.
No breeze.
No-see-ums.

The stress was at an all time high, the islands in a crisis. The curfew was especially a hardship to spend so many dark hot nights in ill comfort. The odor of sewer permeated apartments and houses as people waited until they had some *previously used* water to spare, for flushing the commodes. The air was made hotter, by the candle light and torches people used to light their homes. Quite a few residents stank from lack of proper bathing, the electric water pumps, bringing water up from cisterns below, no longer quietly humming. Mosquitoes hovered around in the airless night. The acrid smell of burning mosquito coils and *Ode d'Off* wafted in the stillness.

A few of the elite were lucky enough to go home to generators. Some even had homes completely intact to enjoy. Their lives made a bit easier with everyday modern conveniences, still at their disposal.

Others were still reeling from the shock of sudden loss of home and job. A few scrambled off the islands to other parts of the globe, but many clung to the rock, so to say, looking for a better day. This too shall pass.

"The Rock" is a nickname for the islands, since they are of volcanic origin. When digging in the dirt, you hit rock and more rock. Building and growing things can be a bit of a challenge with more rock than dirt.

Homeless folks found themselves crowded in with relatives, friends or heaven forbid, the public shelters. Some folks hunted each day before curfew for a secret place to stay that night.

The National Guard was incredibly hostile towards the residents, compounding the stressful situation. Often at curfew, there were traffic jams as people hastened to get home, while the National Guard or police of both stopped traffic while threatening people with arrest. It was a world turned upside down.

For the marine community, life was slightly different. Many folks had lost their boats. It was their only home, for some a lifetime of savings, blown away. Poof. Just like that. A large percentage of people ashore and afloat were uninsured. The cost of living is very high in the Virgins. Insurance was an unaffordable luxury for many boat and home owners.

Much of the live-aboard-floating community, had power and water, some had refrigeration. Many were tied up in hurricane holes, anxious to anchor in a more comfortable place, but afraid of another hurricane. Two in ten days is pretty heady. Each day boats could be seen limping along the seas to the nearest operational boat yard for immediate repairs. Dinghies or professional salvagers were towing some. Quite a few had the looks of hasty repairs, slapped on the hull, to make them seaworthy long enough to make it into the boatyard.

For many this meant traveling through foreign customs and immigration such as the British Virgin Islands. They too had damages, but most of their homes were built to withstand hurricanes, unlike the U.S. neighbors. While utility poles toppled all over St Thomas and St John, Tortola on the British side only had a few to deal with. Power and phones were operational over much of their island. A curfew was unheard of, crime is fairly low year round. BVI residents knew that no government agency would rescue them. They hastened to clean up their island, put roofs back on, erect poles and lines, getting on with business. Their boat yards were doing a record business. Some occupants competed to have a spot in the yard under the bright security night-lights, so they could work in the night, repairing away.

For the live-aboards in both places, life went on much as usual. Many boaters are a self sufficient lot with solar panels and wind generators to power their life with lights, fans, music, movie players, computers and refrigerators. Rain catchers or water makers, those that covert seawater to fresh, enabled them to live a normal life. Propane powered most cooking and some refrigerators.

The curfew meant they too had to go home at night, but could roam the harbor in their dinghies, in search of social interaction. It was common to see a small sailboat with a bevy of dinghies tied up alongside. Often the dinghies had occupants sitting in them, a beer in hand, swapping lies or promoting the coconut tele-graph to people sitting in their own cockpit with their own drink in hand.

Kind of a roving party became common at night as old friendships were savored and new ones forged. Ashore and afloat, gossip had become the number one pastime for an island in crisis with much of their communications and power down.

Some folks previously living ashore were now homeless but staying with friends afloat. Many were beginning to like the self-sufficient float-ing lifestyle. A new breed of boat owners is born after every hurricane while others swear to never-again-in-my-lifetime.

On St John, normally a tranquil island, I polled hurricane victims, asking them;

"How did you cope with the stress after hurricane Luis and Marilyn hurled into your life?"

Here are the replies. Some sad, others comi-cal, all anonymous for obvious reasons. A peek at how folks make do when they must. Many entrusted me with some of their most personal thoughts.

I got drunk every night, especially after cur-few. Home alone in the dark, drinking rum &

rain. That's room temperature rum with room temperature water. If I'm lucky, a squeeze of lime. Funny, I got used to it, sort of. There was nothing else to do. My endless drinks alone, in the dark, no electricity, no running water, a can of beans digesting in my belly, diluted my drunkenness, until I could pass out in the heat of the night.

⊚⊚

I spent a lot of time helping people worse off than me. It made my problems look so insignificant.

⊚⊚

Self-hypnosis. Very relaxing. It relieves my stress.

⊚⊚

I got drunk every night and every day. The hurricane could have been yesterday or last month, it is all a blur to me now. I lost everything in the world.

Except my thirst.

⊚⊚

We smoked a ton of pot. It calmed us down, made us think creatively. We laughed a lot, we felt lucky to be so high and alive!

❦

Well, we did some serious work on our family planning, what with no power or cable TV and the curfew, you know. Well now we're expecting our next child. If she's a girl she will be Marilyn and if a boy he will be Luis. Certainly gives us something bright and hopeful to look forward to!

❦

I clung to my family & friends. I couldn't get enough hugs, shed enough tears, but they were there for me, though a little worse for the wear.

❦

My cats and I became inseparable, I sat in the dark on the floor, night after night, with no furniture, petting them, listening to them purr and let them rub themselves all over me. I had not a stick of furniture left. On the floor I made a palette of such with blankets to sleep on. We all slept in a heap, none of us wanting to be out of touch with the other.

❦

Drugs. Lots of cocaine. I liked to pick up homeless or lonely women & take them home with me before curfew, keeping them all night.

I still had power & water to offer, so it was easy. I got laid a lot.

❧

We're leaving, maybe we'll be back when things are back together, maybe not. This is just not the place to be. I think it is going to get a lot worse before it gets a lot better. I don't want to go, but I don't want to watch the island crumble. Maybe when they get their act together, we will be back. I mean we just bought land here and we're starting to build. But that's later. Maybe we'll be back when it calms down.

❧

Cope with the stress? Well, I really didn't have much stress. My boat made it OK. My cat made it OK. I'm OK. I drink as much now as I did before.

❧

Massages. We took up massaging. At night we'd take turns doing each other. We're thinking of getting married. Our house didn't have much damage. Living by candlelight is kind of romantic. Usually we both work nights, so with this curfew, well it's sort of like an impromptu honeymoon. We've learned a lot more about each other. We have a portable radio but nothing else to really distract us, except our neighbors upstairs. They fight a lot. They scream, they yell, they curse. Perhaps they should take up massaging.

❦

I took up smoking again, after being quit for years. Matter of fact, I took of drinking again. If I had a joint, I'd take up pot again.

❦

I don't have time to deal wit the stress. I get up at four a.m. each day and start working on my house. I am chasing suppliers and workmen down all the time. I've got to get my house back together. When I can't work on the house, I work on the garden. I work all day until I drop into bed exhausted. The curfew doesn't really bother me. I'm at home sleeping early anyhow. We have a generator so we can watch movies. I like to cook, so we eat well.I don't have time to think about the stress.

❦

Before the storm, I harvested all my pot, it was a bit too early, but at least now I have something to smoke the night away.

❧

The beach. We went swimming a lot. We had no jobs and no money. The beaches and swimming are free. It was like pretending to be a tourist. This is a great time to go to the beaches, since there are no tourists anyhow.

❧

Wrote. I just couldn't write enough. I was an insomniac, I wrote half the night and most of the days. Absorbed in my works, it distracted me from my losses. I began carrying paper with me everywhere, some times scribbling on paper bags or bar tabs. My mind was exploding with stories. Or maybe my mind just wanted to escape the reality and delve into my fictional works. Watch out, you could be in my next novel.

❧

Played the piano. I don't have a piano but my friends do. So I stayed at their house so I could play. They suffered through me learning new pieces. It made me feel good, even though I don't play really well, but to learn a new song or play a new tune, like a new future, it gave me hope. Things would get better.

❦❦

Cried. I just cried a lot, I don't deal well with stress at all. This is killing me. I don't know how I am going to go on.

❦❦

Cope with stress! I don't know *how* to cope with the stress, I'm out-a-here soon as the planes start leaving! I've seen enough of this rock! Two hurricanes are more than any lifetime should have to endure!

❦❦

Well, we all partied the night away in the harbor. See we live on a boat and there was no curfew in the harbor, so we would dinghy over to each other's boats and trade rum for coke or food for ice. We had some really good parties in the harbor and lots of hangovers in the morning. It really wasn't that stressful, just a change in my usual evening plans. It's better to live on a boat after a hurricane than ashore. I'd have gone nuts if I had to live the way they do ashore with that curfew and all.

❦❦

Masturbating. Yeah, whenever I got depressed or stressed, I just went home and masturbated.

It may me feel good. Then I could think again, begin to think that maybe there is hope for a brighter tomorrow. My right hand has become my best friend. It relieves me, it distracts me, doesn't have the hassle of a relationship. It put me to rest so I think clearly the next morning.

I play guitar every night. It's about all I have that wasn't wrecked by the hurricane. I don't care if the neighbors like it or not. With nothing much else to do at night, I just play and sing. I'm writing a song about the hurricane blues. I'll play it for you. And he did. Here are his lyrics;

NOTE: WAPA is the local electricity corporation and VITELCO the phone company. Cisterns are regularly used to store water for the home.

Come Blow Away My Hurricane Blues

Hurricane Luis & Marilyn
You blew away my life
You stole my wife
You left me devastated
Come blow away my hurricane blues

Send WAPA out to rekindle my light
Don't leave me in the dark alone

Have VITELCO restore my phone
Don't leave me incommunicado
Come blow away my hurricane blues

Send FEMA out with a tarp for me
Don't leave me out in the rain
Send Red Cross to clothe & feed me
Don't leave me starving naked
Come blow away my hurricane blues

Send the water truck to fill my cistern
Don't leave me thirsty and dirty
Send the cable man to entertain my life
Don't leave me without diversion
Come blow away my hurricane blues

Send my loved ones back to me
Don't leave me alone with no one to love
Send me a job to fill my pockets
Don't leave me with my idle hands
Come blow away my hurricane blues

Send my life back to me
Have my wife running to me
Bring me some good fortune
Something I can weather
Come blow away my hurricane blues

The End

Acknowledgements

My editor wrote this suggested acknowledgement:

This book wouldn't be possible without the help and friendship of so many. First and foremost, I offer my gratitude to …
Secondly, I wish to thank …
(etc.)

So I filled in the blanks:

This book wouldn't be possible without the help and friendship of so many. First and foremost, I offer my gratitude to my readers! Without your constant encouragement I would have never thought this book possible.
Secondly, I wish to thank everyone else!

I realize this isn't what my editor wanted to see.

But, I could easily fill up a whole 'nother book of gratitude.

Continued on next page

So, let me try once more:

First and foremost, I offer my gratitude to my Dear Miss Mermaid readers at StormCarib. Com and at DearMissMermaid.Com. I thank Gert, the webmaster who developed Storm-Carib.Com and all the thoughtful readers who took time to write me words of appreciation and encouragement. I hope your suggestions for me to write down stories and publish books comes up to your expectations.

I've been inspired by thousands of people. Sure there are a few I hold close, very near and dear to my heart, sadly many that inspired me the most, have departed this world, without seeing this book come to fruition.

On one hand I want to thank everyone by name, on the other hand I risk leaving someone out that inspired me during a critical low. Then, quite honestly, there are a few treasured souls, for reasons I wish not to explain, whom I cannot mention publicly, that surely sent me along my way, encouraging my every step.

I love you all and sincerely thank you all from the bottom of my crazy heart and soul.

Dear Miss Mermaid

Made in the USA
Lexington, KY
14 June 2010